the Secret World of
Valarie

the Secret World of
Valarie

Tia Farrell

TATE PUBLISHING
AND ENTERPRISES, LLC

Published by Tate Publishing & Enterprises, LLC
127 E. Trade Center Terrace | Mustang, Oklahoma 73064 USA
1.888.361.9473 | www.tatepublishing.com

Tate Publishing is committed to excellence in the publishing industry. The company reflects the philosophy established by the founders, based on Psalm 68:11,
"The Lord gave the word and great was the company of those who published it."

Book design copyright © 2015 by Tate Publishing, LLC. All rights reserved.
Cover design by Ivan Charlem Igot
Interior design by Jomar Ouano

Published in the United States of America

ISBN: 978-1-68118-888-1
Fiction / Romance / General
15.05.06

CHAPTER 1

Valarie Edwards didn't want to admit that she had an anxiety problem. It wasn't even a problem really, just an irrational fear of almost everything that existed in the world. She was afraid of things such as random nosebleeds, birds swooping down from the sky and attacking her, and unexplainable stomach aches. She was afraid her dad would run out of gas on the side of the road somewhere or get kidnapped and leave her to fend for herself. She was afraid of using the oven, of floods, and swallowing pills. Anything to do with medicine or illness she was afraid of. Most of the stuff she feared was things she had been afraid of since she was a young child. She was only seventeen, and even though her thoughts and fears were irrational, she was well matured for her age, and she had a heart full of compassion.

Valarie often got plenty of chances to face her fears, but she was too afraid of doing that too. Whenever she felt the stress of an anxiety attack coming on, she would run out of her room, down the stairs, out of the house and into the peach orchard that her dad grew and tended to on their twenty acres of land out of the middle of nowhere in Georgia. Past rows and rows of trees she would run, until her legs couldn't carry her anymore or if she tripped over her own feet, whichever one came first.

She didn't think her dad, Tom, knew of her problem. Every day she put on a brave face and smiled at him as he drove her to school on his way to work. She didn't like school, but she was very smart. She had read several books on managing fear, anxiety and stress. She even studied illnesses like cancer, diabetes, and something called muscular dystrophy, but every illness she studied she was afraid she would be sick with it.

Valarie knew sickness. Her mother, Ella, had struggled with cancer since she was six, and the cancer finally won her over four months earlier. That was when she became afraid of hospitals and needles and even doctors. Valarie would have been content to stay at home or in a cardboard box for the rest of her life, hiding from the world and all its dangers. But the law said that she had to complete high school, and she didn't want her dad to go to jail if she became a shut in.

Although her anxiety was a constant battle, the little attacks liked to happen at night while she was trying to relax enough to fall asleep. While she would lie in her bed, reading, she would feel the fear begin to crawl up her spine and sit on top of her head until it turned into dark, scary thoughts. Then her breathing would become shallow, her heart would begin to race and she would jump out of bed in a desperate attempt to calm herself. She kept a notebook in her blue backpack that she would write down every little thing she felt during the day. She would write down the date, time and whatever was bothering hear, whether it was a headache, stomach ache, or twitching of her right eye. Then she would pace across her room, which was actually an old attic her dad converted into a bedroom. If that didn't work, she would slip on her shoes, slowly open her door, quietly race down the stairs, fly out the front door, and run into the orchard. Here is where she would run until she tripped. Mostly she would come to a stop at the thirtieth or fortieth row of trees. At times she would fall to her knees, feeling like she was suffocating and trying to breathe. Other times she would try to keep herself from getting sick. She was afraid of that too. When she regained her breath, and had feeling in her legs again, she would stand and make her way back to the house. She would go back up the stairs into her attic room, drink some water, and lay back down. This always wore her out and she would fall asleep within the hour. It was an exhausting thing to do, and she did it on a daily basis, but she felt that she suffered from an incurable problem. No piece of advice from a book she read or a doctor she met had eased her mind. She felt she was doomed to this life of fear for the rest of her days.

Valarie's alarm clock rang at its usual seven a.m. on a Monday morning in March. She hated getting up early, but it was one of the few things she wasn't afraid of. She got up, got dressed then went into the bathroom to brush her teeth and comb her shoulder-length brown hair. She never styled her hair or wore any makeup, only lip balm when the air felt dry to her skin. Her clothing style was a simple t-shirt and a pair of jeans. She sometimes wore her brown jacket or pale pink sweater whenever it was chilly outside, and as the sun was still trying to warm the cold earth, she chose her ugly brown. She occasionally wore jewelry, but nothing fancy. It was too much work and it took a lot of time out of her mornings to look like a woman from a magazine, plus she didn't really know how to apply makeup. She had never had an interest in those things.

She met her dad downstairs for breakfast and crunched on her cereal while he read the morning paper. She felt sorry for the paper boy who had to go miles and miles past the outskirts of town to get to the orchard every morning just to deliver a bundle of bad news. It wasn't a completely vacant area; the nearest house was an empty bed and breakfast about a mile south of the far right corner of the orchard. The closest living neighbor was two miles after that. The land had belonged to the Edwards' for the past three generations. Valarie's dad had inherited the property from his father as a wedding gift twenty-eight years ago. She had heard the story many times about how he and her mother Ella had continued on with the orchard, tending to the trees and selling its produce for profit. It was a simple life, one her dad said he liked. He said he preferred being in the country to the noise and chaos of a city. Valarie agreed with him. Even though her dad harvested peaches, he still had a day job working as an accountant in the town that was small and quiet. She was glad he was smart in math and could help her with her homework. She didn't want to have to get help from a tutor, was afraid of them.

Her dad had seemed to age several years during the time her mother was sick in the hospital. His gentle face now looked tired all the time, and there was no longer a comforting light in his brown eyes. Grey hairs were scattered in with the black color on his head and in his beard. Valarie couldn't imagine the level of stress losing his wife had put on him. Whenever she asked him how he was feeling, he would put on a smile and say he was feeling better, even though he didn't look it.

After breakfast, the two would get into her dad's truck and drive half an hour to her school where he would leave her on the sidewalk in front of the building.

"I'll be back for you at four," he said, as he would say every morning when he dropped her off near the sidewalk. Valarie was only two months into the semester, yet she was already counting down the days till her graduation next year. After she got out of the truck, she would take a deep breath and venture inside what she would call the scariest place on earth. The halls were busy with kids rushing to get to class or run away from teachers that were walking through the halls. Her locker was a few feet away from the girl's bathroom, giving her the perfect earshot to hear the girls crying to each other about how they didn't make the cheerleading team. Valarie would rather step in dog poop than walk in on a conversation like that.

This year, her first class was English. Not her best subject, but not her worst either. Then came math. She would rather step in dog poop than endure that too. Then gym, which she didn't like because she thought her legs resembled those of a chicken and didn't like wearing shorts, then science, her favorite, then lunch. She didn't like this either because she was afraid of getting food poisoning from the cafeteria food. Then history, which always made her feel sad when she studied the subject, and, lastly, art, which made her feel like she didn't have any artistic talent. Whenever she had a few minutes between classes she would go into the library and find another self-help book to read, one she hoped would give her all the answers as to how to get rid of her "problem." The librarian, Mrs. Saunders, was a nice lady in her late twenties, who knew Valarie by name and always had the next Free Yourself of Anxiety book ready for her to pick up. The woman suggested that she go to the school counselor or talk to an older loved one if she felt that her troubles were too much for her to handle, but Valarie simply shook her head and said that the reading was for academic purposes. She didn't want anyone to know that she was afraid of counselors and therapy.

When her day at school was done, she would wait outside for her dad to come pick her up. He would ask how her day was and she would say her day was fine and ask him the same question. He would talk about a client or an equation he solved for his boss because his boss couldn't solve it because his boss failed algebra in college yet somehow got an accounting degree. Then they would go inside their home, cook some dinner, eat and sit in the living room together while Valarie did her homework and her dad read or watched TV. Then they would go to their bedrooms for the night and Valarie would spend the night fighting her inner fears while her dad slept peacefully. Being afraid of everything made her feel like she was drowning, yet she didn't want to call out for help because she didn't want anybody to know think she was stupid or crazy. She was sinking.

Valarie awoke a few minutes before her alarm went off. Yet she stayed in bed until its beeping tone screamed at her and rang in her ears. She went about her normal morning routine, breakfast, and the ride to school no differently than she had done the past four months.

"I'll be back at four," her dad said, as she climbed out of his truck. She shut the door then paused to wave good-bye.

After he drove off, she turned to face her rival. She stood on the sidewalk a little longer than usual. She noticed the sun shining a little brighter, and that it felt good on her light skin. As she looked at the sun shining on her bare arm, she realized she hadn't been getting much sun at all. Her skin was whiter than a marshmallow, and almost as squishy to the touch. But she didn't plan on getting a tan any time soon, she was afraid of sunburn turning into skin cancer.

She walked into the building, avoiding eye contact with everyone as usual, and made her way to English class. She froze as she walked into the classroom and saw someone in her seat near the back row. She didn't like sitting up front. She was afraid of being called on to answer a question she didn't know the answer to. A boy about her age, with blonde hair that sat just above his neck line, was sitting in her seat, talking to Eric, the kid who sat next to her. She knew everyone's name in class just by listening to the teacher call on them. Valarie wasn't sure whether to ask him to move or to simply find another seat, but the only free seat was one in the front, and she wasn't going to sit up there. She slowly and cautiously approached the kid and cleared her throat. He didn't hear her. She cleared her throat again, this time louder. He turned to her and smiled a big smile revealing all white teeth. Valarie noticed that his blue eyes sparkled.

"What's up?" he asked in a casual voice, as if he was her best friend.

She hesitated, not knowing how to sound, not really knowing how to talk to a stranger and not sound stupid.

"This is my seat," she stuttered.

The kid's smile faded. "Oh, my bad, I can move." He started to gather his books.

Eric put his hand on the desk. "Don't worry about it," he said to the new kid. "She can take the seat up front." His dark eyes were beginning to look irritated.

"No, dude, it's cool. If she was here first she has a right to the seat." He grabbed his bag and rose to his feet. He faced her. "All yours," he said, smiling again. "I'm David, by the way." He held out his hand to her.

For a moment she stared at him, then at his hand. She didn't want to shake it. She was afraid of germs. Yet she knew it was the polite thing to do. She slowly lifted her hand and cautiously placed it in his. She could feel his light skin against hers, almost stinging as if he was burning her with his touch. She didn't like the feeling.

David stared at her as if he was waiting for something. Then she noticed that she hadn't introduced herself. "I'm Valarie," she said, in a robotic tone. She wanted to run and hide.

He shook her hand roughly then dropped it. He turned back to Eric and said, "See you at lunch." Then he made his way to the front seat.

Valarie sat down, relieved that she had gotten her seat back, but feeling like she made a fool of herself to the new kid. He was probably already thinking that she was a stupid one to stay away from. At the same time, she thought she just might have died if she sat any closer to the teacher.

"Just my luck," Eric sighed under his breath.

Valarie looked away and hid her face. She wanted to disappear.

Valarie made her way through the lunch line in a matter of minutes then went to sit at a table in the back of the cafeteria where no one would see her. It was her favorite table to sit at because it was always empty and deserted. No other students liked sitting in the back so Valarie had the table all to herself every day. She pulled out her latest self-help book and began to read. She was halfway through her lunch when she heard someone say her name.

"Hey, Valarie, want to come sit with us?" David was standing several feet from the table with Eric, both of them on their way to a table up front. David stared at her as he waited for her response. They were both carrying lunch trays.

"I'm all right here," she said awkwardly.

"Are you sure?" David asked.

Eric nudged his arm with his elbow. "She said she's fine. Let's go get a good seat by the window."

David stood where he was, waiting for her to answer.

"I'm sure," she said. She didn't want Eric to become any more irritated than he already was.

"All right, I'll see you later then," David said. He and Eric went to the far side of the cafeteria near the windows, and Valarie could see him look back at her every so often. She soon felt that he was looking at her too much. She put her book in her bag and took her tray to the counter up front, then hurried out of the cafeteria before her breathing got too shallow. *Stupid kid*, she thought, *trying to invite me to sit with them. Who does he think he is? He's messing up my usual dull and unsociable day.* The rest of the school day dragged on without any more interruptions from the new kid.

After Valarie got ready for bed, she pulled her book out of her bag and tried not to think about lunch earlier that day. David seemed to be a weird kid. Why had he been so nice? Everyone else just avoided her, as if she was invisible. What was it about David that made him see her? Was something changing with her? Was her invisibility wearing off? Would more people begin to socialize with her?

The questions made her heart feel like it was fluttering. She pulled out her illness notebook and quickly wrote down her symptoms. Then she took a few deep breaths.

He's just a weird kid, she told herself, trying to calm her thoughts. *But what if he talks to me again tomorrow? What if he sits with me at lunch? What if this goes on and on for days?*

The air in her room became stuffy and hot. She went over to window and opened it all the way. She felt as if she couldn't breathe. She slipped her shoes on and did her usual mad dash out of the house. Down the steps and into the trees she ran until she couldn't go anymore. She fell down to her knees and tried to regain her breath.

Curse that kid! she thought. *He's already causing me too much agony.*

"Hey?" a voice said.

She jumped onto her feet at the sound of someone nearby. A beam of light shone on her shirt and a figure was walking toward her from the corner of the field.

"Are you okay?" the voice asked.

She would have turned and ran away, but the voice was strangely familiar. She tried to see past the light, but she couldn't until the figure got closer to her. The light went from her shirt to her feet, making it easier for her to see who was talking.

"Valarie? Do you live here?"

It was David.

CHAPTER 2

Valarie felt a lump grow in her throat as David stood a few feet away from her.

"This is my dad's orchard," she stuttered.

David nodded his head. "That's cool. I'm glad I know who my neighbors are."

Valarie thought she had heard him wrong. "We're neighbors?"

"Yeah, my parents and I moved into the bed and breakfast a mile down the road that way," he pointed to the way which he came from with his flashlight.

The lump in Valarie's throat felt as if it was growing larger. *The weird kid is my neighbor? How could that happen?* Now she wouldn't be able to escape him, even at home.

"Oh," she said. The sound of disappointment in her voice was evident.

"Are you okay? It looked like you fell or something," David asked, pointing his flashlight downward. Valarie could see that he wasn't smiling his usual smile, which made her feel a bit more uncomfortable.

"I…uh…was looking for something," she said. It was the first thing that came to her mind and as soon as she said it, she realized that it sounded stupid.

"Looking for something in the dark?" he asked, drawing out his words in disbelief.

Valarie looked around and remembered that it was almost ten o'clock at night. Then she looked down at herself. She was in her teddy bear-printed pajamas.

"Um," she said, trying to think of something else to say. Her breathing was getting shallow again. She tried to calm down herself enough to give David a believable answer. He was staring at her, waiting for her to speak. She felt like she had become a bug under a microscope. Without thinking, Valarie turned and ran back through the orchard toward her home. She made it to the front porch, jumped up the steps two at a time, and swung open the door. She forgot that her dad was sleeping until after she had slammed the door behind her in a desperate attempt to hide. She waited for her dad to come out and ask what was going on, but he never did. Valarie would swear he could sleep through a hurricane. She leaned back against the door and stood there for a long time, thinking about how stupid and childish she had just acted. David was simply trying to be nice and she ran away from him. Boy, how she hated her anxiety! She would have stood and talked with him if she had only known how to be social without acting stupid. Now how would she face him at school after the way she acted? *Maybe he won't show up tomorrow?* she thought. *Or maybe he would and ask me if I was okay.* Valarie slapped a hand to her forehead. She had never felt more stupid in her life.

The next morning, Valarie almost wanted to tell her dad that she didn't feel good enough to go to school. But if she did, he would worry about her all day, and give her medicine and maybe even take her to the doctor. What a dilemma she was up against! Who was easier to face, the doctor or David? Which one would be less painful? The doctor would tell her she was fine. She didn't know what David would say. Still, she couldn't sum up the courage to back out of school. Besides, she was afraid of staying home alone. She might as well go to school.

She stood outside the building trying to resist the urge to run away. Maybe she could just ignore David. Maybe he would ignore her. Why was she so worried about it? *Stop this!* she told herself, *you're acting like a child.* She tried to get her feet to move, but she felt as if she was wearing lead shoes. She knew that if she didn't move soon she would be late for class, and she didn't want every one staring at her as she made her way to the back of the classroom after the teacher had already started his lecture.

Valarie closed her eyes and bit her lip. Then she forced herself to move one foot in front of the other until she got to her classroom. She walked in just in time for Mr. Collins to tell his class to pay attention, and she was able to slip into the back unnoticed, though she had the feeling David noticed her. After she seated herself, she noticed he didn't turn around to look at her, which made her feel that she had made him uncomfortable the night before. *Of course you did, stupid*, she thought, *you ran away from the guy. Are we going to be doing this all day?*

Valarie dreaded lunch more than sitting with him through their first class. Now David had the opportunity to talk to her, and he was probably going to ask her what it was that made her run away from him. She sat at her usual empty table in the back of the cafeteria and reached into her bag for her book. It was gone. Then she remembered that she forgot to pack it that morning, she was too busy worrying about what David would say to her. Now she had nothing to read and worse yet, she wouldn't look busy for someone to strike up a conversation. Instead she pulled out her English notebook and began to go over the day's notes. Her assignment come finals week was to write about someone who inspired her. That was going to be a challenge. The only person she ever knew well enough to be inspired by was her parents. The other kids would probably pick some movie star in one of those vampire movies she tried to avoid. Yet to her, the person who inspired her the most was her mom. She thought about those long days at the hospital when her mom was struggling to survive. Valarie had continued school on and on those few months before her mother's death. She was glad her dad let her take that Friday off to spend the day with her, for that night she had died. Valarie still found it hard to talk about her mother's death with her dad. She was afraid of opening up to people.

A lunch tray was placed on the table, bringing Valarie back to the present, and almost making her jump out of her seat.

"Sorry, I didn't mean to scare you," David said, taking the seat next to her as if she had invited him. She suddenly felt very self-conscious. She caught the scent of his body spray, and for a second she thought the scent was pleasant.

"How are you today?" he asked, picking up his fork and digging in to whatever casserole was on his plate.

"I'm all right."

"Did you ever find what you were looking for last night?" he asked, with a strange look in his eye, as if he thought the whole thing was funny.

"About that—" Valarie started to explain.

"Hey, don't worry about it," David said with his usual smile. "I didn't mean to scare you."

"It wasn't you, I just…" She couldn't find a reason to tell him why she had run away. *What should I tell him?* she asked herself. *I have terrible anxiety that makes it hard for me to talk to people? Sure, so I can sound even weirder than I do now.*

David was staring at her, waiting for her to finish her sentence.

"I'm sorry," she said, trying to get the conversation off the subject.

"It's all right," he said. He continued eating as if he wasn't bothered at all.

It is? Valarie thought. *That's all? That was easier than I thought. All that worrying this morning was for nothing. Maybe David wasn't so weird a kid after all.*

"So, do you have any ideas about who you're going to write your final paper on?" David asked, changing the subject. He had already cleaned his plate of the casserole and started drinking his tall glass of water.

Valarie cleared her throat. She was glad the subject was off of her, but the question made her think of her mother. "I have one. What about you?" she said quickly.

He set his empty glass down and wiped his mouth with his napkin. "No. I'm usually a really bad procrastinator. I'll probably end up writing the whole paper the night before it's due."

Valarie tried to smile, despite her urge to tell him how unprofessional procrastination was. So far the conversation had been casual, yet she was fighting the urge to run away again.

David had finished his lunch and was staring at Valarie, as if he expected her to say something. She looked down at her half eaten plate. Suddenly she wasn't hungry anymore.

"So…." she said, trying to fill the awkward silence. "How do you like Georgia?" She was surprised with herself. She had actually gotten up the nerve to ask someone's opinion about something. Normally she was afraid of talking to people for more than two minutes. *This David kid sure brings out the weird in me*, she thought. *Maybe he's just a bad influence.*

"It's just another town where people talk funny," he answered with a sarcastic smile. Then he shrugged his shoulders. "Honestly, it's just another school."

Valarie grew curious. "How many high schools have you been to?"

"This would be my third. My parents are lawyers, and a few years back they got offered a job in Colorado, so we lived there for a while till…" his voice trailed off, as if he was thinking of a memory he didn't want to talk about. "Then we came here."

Valarie nodded. "Oh," she said, feeling the awkward tension.

"What do your parents do?" he asked.

"My dad is an accountant. My mother…passed away…a few months ago." She stuttered those last few words.

"I'm sorry," David said. He seemed to feel sympathetic, which made her uncomfortable. She didn't like people feeling sorry for her, especially when it came to her mother's death.

"Do you have any brother or sisters?" he asked.

"No."

"I have one brother. He's in Hawaii."

"Really?" she asked, her eyes widening. She had always admired Hawaii for its beautiful scenery and wildlife. She would have given anything to spend a day on the island.

"Yeah. He works in one of those turtle aquariums. He sends me pictures all the time of the ocean and the tide pools. It makes me so jealous. I want to go there so badly and stand in the warm sand. Maybe even hold a turtle."

"It sounds nice," Valarie said. She could picture the ocean in her mind, with beige sand under her feet and blue sky overhead. Suddenly she realized how much she had been talking in the past ten minutes. It was probably much more than she had said all week. *Am I actually having a civilized conversation?* she asked herself. *And I haven't ran away or thrown up? This is great!* She smiled without realizing it.

"Hey," David said, his face softening and his eyes sparkling. "A smile. I was beginning to think your face was broken."

Valarie frowned. She didn't know if it was an insult or a compliment.

"That was a joke," David said. He must have noticed her confusion.

Valarie could feel her face grow hot. *Am I blushing?* She normally blushed when she felt embarrassed, but the weird kid had actually complimented her.

"You have a nice smile. You should wear it more often, Valarie."

The sound of her name from his mouth made her spine tingle. Many people had said her name, but so far no one said it the way he did. He made it sound special and beautiful, almost as if he liked it. Suddenly her chest began to feel tight and she knew that a panic attack was coming.

"I have to go," she said. She shoved her book in her bag and stood up. For a second she stood there staring at his confused expression. For a second she thought about sitting down and continuing to talk with him, but instead she turned and silently left the cafeteria. She made her way down the hall and entered the girl's bathroom. She went into a stall, dropped her backpack, and sat on the seat of the toilet. She didn't notice that she was crying until she tasted salt on her lips.

CHAPTER 3

That evening, Valarie sat at the kitchen table across from her dad as the two ate their dinner. The truck ride home had consisted of him talking about his day while Valarie listened, or tried to listen. Her mind had drifted back to the cafeteria and the look on David's face when he told her she had a nice smile. Her heart fluttered every time she thought about it, which made her want to forget it.

Even though Valerie usually told her dad about the little things that happened during her day at school, she hadn't told him about David. Not because she was afraid that her dad would over react about her meeting a boy, but because she wasn't sure how she felt about him. She didn't want to believe that he liked her. After all, no one liked her. She was too quiet and reserved for anyone to put up with her. It was easier for everyone, including herself, to just leave her alone. She was invisible, and she was all right with that. How did David see her? What did he see her as? Some helpless little girl who was too weird and awkward to fit in? *That's what I am after all*, she told herself. She didn't want David to change that. She had gotten along by herself just fine before he came along. He didn't need to go talking to her and liking her, trying to change the fact that she was alone in high school. She didn't want anything to change. She was afraid of change.

"Is something wrong with the pasta, Val?"

Her dad's voice brought her out of her thoughts and back to the table. She looked down at her plate and realized that she had only taken a few bites. "No. I was just… thinking."

"What about?" he asked, in between bites.

Valarie hesitated. She didn't want to tell him about David, much less talk about him. She wanted to forget the whole thing, as if it was a bad dream. "My final paper," she said quietly. Then she felt a churn in her stomach from not telling him the truth. "I have to write about someone who has inspired me."

Tom took a drink of his sweet tea then put his cup down. "Final paper? Didn't the semester just start?"

"Yeah. My teacher just wants us to start thinking about it."

"That shouldn't be hard. You like writing."

"Yeah," Valarie admitted, even though she wouldn't tell that to anyone. She was afraid of people reading her work. "I just can't think of anyone to write about."

He took his last bite then stood and took his plate to the sink. "You'll find somebody."

"Who would you say has inspired you?" she asked.

Valarie watched as her dad turned on the water and plugged the sink. He added soap and the dishes from dinner. Valarie could tell he was thinking. "There are a lot of people who've inspired me Val," he said in a tone so soft Valarie wondered if he was crying. "If I had to pick one, I'd say that person would be my mom."

I'd say my mom too, she thought. She didn't say anymore on the subject, instead she finished her meal in silence. Just as she ate her last bite and took her plate to the sink, a knock came at the front door. Her dad left the sink to answer the call and Valarie took over washing the dishes. She heard the front door squeak open and the sound of muffled voices floated into the kitchen. She could make out her dad's voice, the other sounded young, yet quiet. Probably some kid trying to sell something to raise money for his school. She gathered a handful of silverware to set in the drain board and she pulled the plug for the sink. The front door closed. The sound of footsteps grew closer as her dad came back into the kitchen.

"Valarie," she heard him say.

She turned around and dropped the handful of silverware at the sight of David standing behind her dad, his backpack over his shoulder. *Oh no, he's in my house!* she thought. She felt a knot twist in her stomach. She slowly bent down to pick up the dishes, her eyes still stuck on David.

"Hey," he said, smiling.

"You have a visitor," Tom said.

Valarie quickly turned and dropped the silverware back in the sink.

"Well, actually, I came to see you, sir," David said, turning toward her father. "I remember Valarie telling me that you're an accountant, and I was wondering if you would be willing to help me with some math homework. I'll pay you of course."

Please say no, Dad, she thought, *please say no*. David standing in her house gave her a nervous feeling, like standing in front of a crowd with thousands of eyes on her.

"Well, I don't see why not. But you can keep your money. Any friend of my daughter's is a friend of mine." The look on Tom's face was like that of a kid on Christmas. Valarie could just hear his thoughts; my poor, shy daughter has finally found a friend that's not four legged! Her face began to grow hot, this time she knew it was from embarrassment.

"We can sit here at the table. I got an idea, Val, why don't you pull out your homework so I can help you both at the same time?"

David looked more than thrilled at the idea. "Great," he said.

Her stomach twisted again and she hoped she wouldn't be sick. Without saying a word, she walked out of the kitchen and retrieved her backpack from the table near the front door. She looked at the door for a second and thought about running away. She didn't want to do her homework with David, it's not like he was her friend or anything. The stupid kid just liked to pick on her and embarrass her. They would notice if she ran away. Maybe not at first, but eventually. *Maybe I could fake a stomach ache. Well, at this point, I wouldn't have to fake it. What if I—*

"Are you coming, Val?" her dad called from the kitchen. She groaned and forced herself to go back to the table. David had pulled out his books and set his backpack near the head of the table. As he saw her, he pulled out the chair next to his, motioning for her to sit by him. Her limbs felt numb as she took the seat. As she scooted closer to the table, she looked up at her dad. He was still smiling. Valarie couldn't remember the last time he had smiled so big for so long.

David sat and she could feel her heart began to flutter as it had earlier. She hoped no one could hear it, even though it was pounding in her own ears. They both watched her as she pulled out her math homework. She hadn't glanced at it since fourth period, and looking at it now, she realized it was simple algebra, work she could have completed in twenty minutes. She wondered if David really had trouble with it, or if he just used it as an excuse to come pick on her.

"Let's see what we have here," Tom said, taking Valarie's worksheet. He was still smiling.

"Thanks for all your help, sir," David said, packing up his books.

"Anytime. And no more of this 'sir' stuff, you can call me Tom."

David smiled. Valarie noticed his eyes sparkle.

"Val, why don't you walk him out?" her dad said.

Valarie's stomach dropped.

"That's all right sir, uh, Tom, I'll let myself out." David threw his bag over his shoulder.

"It's the polite thing to do for our guest," he said, still looking at Valarie.

She was silent for a moment, staring at her dad and wondering if he was joking. But she did as she was told. She walked to the front door while David thanked her dad again. Then the two made their way down the steps toward the orchard.

"We can cut through here," Valarie said, leading him into the peach trees.

"Your dad's a nice guy," David said after a moment of silence.

Valarie nodded. "He's a good man. He deserves more than what he's got."

"What do you mean?"

"All he has is me. I'm not exactly a prize kid."

David stopped in his tracks. He reached up and gently touched a bud on the tree. "It doesn't matter what you are or what you earn, if you love him and respect him he has all he needs. Being who you are is more than enough, Valarie."

If only you knew who I am, she thought. Then she started to argue with herself that she didn't want him to truly know who she was inside.

"So this becomes a peach, huh?"

Valarie nodded, even though he wasn't looking at her.

"How long do they take to grow?"

"They start to bloom in the spring. They're not ripe until late summer."

"Can you pick them right off the branch and eat them?"

Valarie wondered how a tiny peach had captured his attention. Maybe he wasn't as smart as she thought he was. "Sure, when they're ripe and ready."

"Do you get to eat them?"

She nodded again.

"Cool. Free peaches."

Valarie suppressed a giggle. This kid was an air head.

They made their way to the end of the property in silence. Valarie stopped abruptly. "I guess I'll see you tomorrow," she said.

"All right. Thanks," David said. He smiled one more time before continuing on his way home.

Thank God it's Friday, Valarie thought. *Maybe I can get a break from you over the weekend.* She made her way back through the orchard and went inside the house. Her dad was sitting on the couch with a book in his hand.

"So, when were you going to tell me about our new neighbors?" He turned to look at her with his same excited smile.

"I…forgot," she said.

"Sure," her dad said in a teasing sort of voice. "You forgot to tell me about a boy your age that you go to school with and who seems to like you a bit. I bet every teenage girl forgets something like that."

Valarie sighed. She had tried to avoid this talk. "I'm sorry."

He waved his hand as if waving it off. "He seems like a nice kid." He turned back to his book.

"I guess so," Valarie said. She headed toward the kitchen for her backpack.

"I'm glad you got a study buddy."

"Is that what you called them in your day?" she hollered from the table.

"Yep. What do you kids call them now? A boyfriend?"

Valarie sighed again. "I don't have time for a boyfriend." She took her bag and sat on the other end of the couch to finish the rest of her homework.

"I'll agree with you there," Tom said. He suddenly looked disappointed, almost sad. "I think you spend too much time here, Val," he said. "You're a good kid. You need to be with kids your age."

Valarie wondered where his concern was coming from. "I'm just fine here," she said.

"That may be the problem." He paused for a moment, then went on, "You deserve so much better than this."

Valarie almost laughed. "I'm fine, Dad. Really. Don't worry about me."

"I'm the dad, it's my job to worry."

"Well, you're overworked and underpaid."

Her dad smiled, but his eyes still looked sad. He turned back to his book and left Valarie to her homework.

CHAPTER 4

Valarie didn't bother pulling out her latest self-help book to read during lunch time the next day. She had come to expect David to sit with her shortly after she sat down to eat. The two ended up talking about school assignments, and what it was like to live on a peach orchard.

Saturday was quiet for Valarie. She stayed home for most of the day, occasionally going outside to get some fresh air. There was no sign of David at his house, which Valarie would see if she walked to the far end of the orchard near the property line. She didn't know why she was checking to see if he was home. *A day free of that kid will do me some good*, she told herself. Finally around four o'clock, she got her book and went to sit out on the porch to read. She read until her dad called her in for dinner, and the rest of the day passed uneventfully, until eleven that night when her daily panic attack took hold and she ran outside like a mad man. She had gotten back up on her feet before she saw the beam of light a few yards away.

"Is this a nightly thing with you?" David asked. He had a sarcastic smile on his face.

Valarie pushed some hair behind her ears. "You could say that." She tried to catch her breath. "What are you doing out here?" she answered, feeling a little hostile.

David waved his flashlight. "I like walking at night. It's quiet and peaceful. Plus I like stargazing."

Valarie looked up. Twinkling stars were scattered across the sky like glitter on a black piece of paper. She had never taken the time to notice it before. She was always too busy trying to regulate her breathing and her heart rate whenever see came out at night.

"So what brings you out?" David asked.

Valarie looked back at the kid, thinking about the anxiety that felt so strong she had to run outside just to reduce its affects. "I needed some fresh air," she told him.

Suddenly the sound of small yapping came from behind him. A little dog, no taller than a foot high was bounding toward her, making his presence known long before he arrived.

"Tiny! Get beck inside," he ordered in a gentle voice, but the dog ran right up to Valarie in excitement. She bent down to pet her, and saw that she was a young golden retriever. Her burnt orange color was beautiful and her long fur was soft as silk. "She's so cute." Valarie smiled as the dog continuously licked her face and arms.

"She's just a big attention hog." David said. He bent down and ruffled Tiny's fur. "Aren't you? Aren't you an attention hog?" he cooed.

Valarie stopped petting the dog when she noticed that David was staring at her. His eyes were transfixed on her face. *What are you thinking?* She wanted to ask him. Instead she stood up, feeling too close to him for comfort.

David petted his dog some more before standing. "Are you hungry?" he asked.

Valarie looked puzzled. "It's almost midnight," she said, thinking that it was too late to eat anything.

"Yeah, and I ate like, six hours ago. I'm starved," he said with a grin.

The laugh she was trying to hold back came out.

"Come on," he said, motioning her to follow him. He turned around and started toward his house, aiming his flashlight at the trees.

Valarie's smile dropped. "Where are we going?" she asked, getting anxious again.

"To my house. You want something to snack on?" he called over his shoulder.

She hesitated. "What about your parents?"

David stopped and turned to her. "They're asleep. It's all right. We'll just sit on the porch so we don't wake them. If you want to join me, that is." He continued on to his house.

Valarie heard the voice of reason shouting at her in her head. *Don't follow him! You don't know what he's thinking or planning to do!* She felt tempted to run home.

David stopped and pointed his flashlight at her. "Are you coming?" he asked. He must have seen the concern on her face for he said, "It's all right Val. I just thought you'd like some company."

She stared at him for a moment, then looked down at Tiny who sat at her master's feet. Her eyes were soft and almost sad, as if she was pleading for Valarie to join them. Feeling like her shoes were filled with cement, she took one step, then another until she caught up with him, and the two made their way up the small hill to his house, Tiny walking along beside them. The house was much like hers, wooden, old, yet less weather worn, as if someone had given it a polish recently.

"You can sit down. I'll go in and get us some food." He waved at a porch swing then silently walked inside. Valarie wondered if he left the door unlocked whenever he went walking at night. She could have lectured him on how unsafe that was. She sat down, trying to keep her breathing slow and steady. She didn't know if she should be there, especially without her dad's permission, but as long as it was just a quick snack then back to bed she thought it would be fine. Something bumped her knee and she noticed that Tiny had sat at her feet, still wanting attention. She couldn't help but smile as she petted the dog.

David came out almost ten minutes later with a plate of cut fruits and a bag of chocolate-covered pretzels. He set them down on the bench between them. "My parents are pretty healthy eaters, so I don't get much junk food." He went back inside and came out a few seconds later with two tall cups of sweet tea. He gave one to Valarie then sat and started eating. She hesitated before she took a pretzel and began to munch. Tiny had left her feet and went to the center of the porch and lay down, resting her head on her paws. She let out a long sigh.

"This is nice," David said, "hanging out outside of school. I don't know about you, but sometimes I'd rather be anywhere but there."

"I like learning," Valarie said. Then she felt like a nerd after she said it.

"I thought so. You're always reading and always studying. What else do you like to do?"

She swallowed hard and thought about what other activities she filled her days with. "Nothing really. I don't do much of anything else."

David drank half his cup of tea before speaking. "I like video games, and building car models."

Valarie had never done either in her life. Suddenly she was very much aware of how boring her life seemed on the outside looking in.

"What do you like to read? I noticed you read a lot of self-help or how to overcome various issues."

Valarie nodded. She didn't really know how to explain why she read all those books, and she didn't like anyone asking her either.

"If you don't mind me asking, what is it that you suffer from?"

Valarie almost choked. "What makes you say that I suffer from something?"

David lowered his hand with a grape still in his fingers. "Don't tell me you read all that stuff for fun?"

Valarie was silent.

"You are trying to find a way to help yourself, yes?"

Valarie nodded, like a child who admitted she stole a cookie from the jar.

"What is it that you're sick with?" he asked again.

Valarie breathed in deep. She couldn't say it. How could she say it? She would sound so stupid. He would laugh at her, and find her weirder than she already made herself out to be. She couldn't tell him, could she? He already saw that she was reading those books for advice to apply to her own life, maybe he would understand.

She opened her mouth to answer, yet the words wouldn't come out. She had never told anyone else before, and it was hard just to find her voice to speak the words.

"It's all right; you don't have to tell me." He popped the grape in his mouth.

"I'm afraid I'll sound stupid," she said, not knowing what else to say.

"It'll only sound stupid if it is stupid." He said. "The way I see it, is you have an issue, just like every other human being on this planet. No one is perfect, we all have flaws." David sounded so smart, almost like he knew what she wanted to hear. Her arms went numb as she braced herself.

"I have…I have anxiety."

Valarie started as David gasped. Her wide eyes were fixed on him, waiting to see what his deal was. Suddenly he burst out laughing.

"I'm sorry," he said, catching his breath. "I'm just messing with you." His laugh was sincere and contagious. Valarie couldn't help but laugh with him.

"Anxiety. That's nothing new," he said, once he caught his breath.

"It's anxiety that makes me afraid of everything." She continued. "Most of what I'm afraid of is just irrational." She paused, not knowing why she had confessed it.

"Like what?" David asked, setting his empty cup down near his feet. He turned to Valarie and focused on her as if she was telling a good story.

"Like cloudy water. Like birds that have long beaks. Like crickets attacking my window."

"Crickets? Little, harmless crickets? Get out of here." He obviously didn't believe her.

"See, it's all just stupid." Valarie could see that he was trying not to laugh. She didn't know whether to laugh with him or feel offended.

"You know something; I used to be the exact same way."

Valarie brightened. "Really?"

"Really. I used to be so scared of thunderstorms and rain that I would hide in the bathroom for hours. I was also afraid of riding in the car because I didn't want to get carsick."

A wave of relief swept over Valarie, like water out of a facet, running down her skin. "I was beginning to think I was the only one," she confessed.

David shook his head. "That's the oldest lie in the book, Valarie. You're never alone. Whatever you are suffering from, someone somewhere is suffering from it too. There is only one you, but there are thousands of fears that feed off of thousands of people every day."

Valarie hesitated. David seemed to know all about anxiety, and she wondered if he had once searched for the answers that she was trying to find. She swallowed hard and asked the question that had plagued her mind for months. "How do you get rid of it?"

David looked down at his feet then back at her. "Fear is just an illusion. You're afraid because somebody told you to be afraid of something or you saw something bad happen to someone and are afraid it will happen to you. It's just an alertness of what you don't want to experience, and sometimes we dwell on it way too much. You can't think about it all the time or else it will start to take over your life. That kind of stress will make you sick. If something is going to happen you can't stop it from happening, so why be afraid of it? Being afraid isn't going to change anything, expect keep you in a box for the rest of your life, and that's no way to live."

"Does it ever go away?"

"Yeah, it does. But you got to work through it. Tell it who's boss. Tell it that it doesn't run your life. You run your life, and as long as you believe that, believe what you tell yourself, you can do anything. The mind is a powerful thing Valarie. You can convince yourself into doing anything."

She took a moment to let his words sink in. Then she asked, "How did you get through it?"

David let out a laugh. "For me, it was getting to the point where I couldn't leave my house. I finally had enough. I was so young and all the advice in the world wasn't helping. I needed to change my outlook if I wanted to change my life. Another thing that helped was getting some spiritual guidance. My poor heart and soul was so anxious that I almost caused an ulcer in my stomach. After months of Bible reading and prayer, I had to give it all to a Higher Being. I had to give it up and be done with it, and truly give it up with no take backs. I had to give it over to Someone who I knew was powerful enough to take it away and make my life the way it's supposed to be. I'm not overly religious, but I do believe in God and that He helped ease my fears. It's the only thing I'm sure of when I get scared."

Valarie listened with her full attention. Everything David said, all the practical reasons as to why she was so anxious and what she could do about it was more advice than what she had gotten from any of those self-help books. She almost wished she knew him sooner so she could have started applying his wisdom to her life.

"That thing you do every night, running out into your orchard, that's anxiety driven, isn't it?"

Valarie felt her eyes grow wide. "How did you know?"

David smiled and his eyes sparkled in the porch light. "I used to do the same thing. The anxiety felt so strong inside that I thought I was going to throw up. So to let it all out, I took to running. It tires out the mind and body and leaves no more energy for anxious thoughts. Of course, running for sport was much more helpful than running at one o'clock in the morning."

The two were quiet for a moment, as Valarie was thinking of all he had said. She knew she needed to let her anxiety go, but how? "How do you let it go?"

"Well, the first thing I did was try not to think about it so much," David said, shifting on the seat. "No one needs that kind of negativity on their mind every second of every day."

"I've tried to do that. I've tried to block out all the thoughts over and over and the next thing I know is I'm thinking about it all over again."

"Did you let all the thoughts go? Did you truly let it go? Or did you say you did then go back to worrying about it as soon as you turned around?"

Valarie thought for a moment. All those times of letting go never made her feel any better. She always felt like there was some key word or phrase she would have to speak, like a password, in order for her thoughts to go away, yet she could never find the key answers. She felt that without the answer she was doomed to hold onto it all for forever. *Does one just simply say 'I let it go' and be done with it? Was it that easy?*

"I guess I don't really know how to do it," she said.

"There's no special way of doing it, Valarie. Just simply let it go."

"Let it go? Just like that?" she asked in disbelief.

"Just like that," David confirmed.

"That doesn't work for me," she said.

"You may not feel better at first. But once you let it go, don't pick it up. Do it once and be done."

"What if it comes back?" she asked.

"Don't let it in. It doesn't control you anymore. It has no place in your mind now."

Valarie took in his every word. It all seemed to make sense, yet it felt like it would be the hardest thing to apply to her life. She looked at David, studied his face, and for the first time since she met him, she saw the lines under his eyes, as if they were marks from a time of stress. "How old are you?" she asked.

"Eighteen."

"And how do you know all this?"

He smiled again. "I was a lot like you a few years ago. I read and researched all I could on this burden of mine, till I finally gave up. I gave it all up, the worry, the fear, the stress. And sooner or later, I started facing all those fears. Some things still get to me to this day, but I got to remind myself who's boss, me or the fear?"

Valarie suddenly became envious of his easy outlook on life. She suddenly wanted to be like him and have a worry-free day for once.

"Don't stress yourself out, Valarie. You're in control. Tell the fear who's boss, leave it on the side of the road, and don't look back."

Valarie nodded, letting him know that she understood. David offered her the last pretzel from the bag. Valarie shook her head. She watched as David popped the pretzel in his mouth and crumpled the bag. Tiny lifted her head in curiosity. "Not for you," David told her in a gentle voice. The dog laid her head back down on her paws and sighed once again. David nodded toward the dog. "She's got such a rough life."

CHAPTER 5

Valarie woke up the next morning with a mission. She resolved to tell her fear who was boss, and let it all go, just like David had said. After he had walked her home the night before, she felt a sense of realization, and wanted to apply this new attitude to her life. She figured it was worth a shot since everything else she had tried in the past had failed. She had always heard of the "If I can do it, you can do it!" phrase, but when David explained it, it all made better sense. Maybe this time, she really could do it. Perhaps she just needed to hear it face to face from someone's mouth, not just reading the words on a page.

She wondered how she had met someone with whom she could finally share her fears with and learn about how to manage them. David knew so much and had been through the same problem already. Of course, he had mentioned that his belief in God had helped him out. Valarie didn't know what to think when it came to God or religion. She and her parents used to go to church every Sunday, but after her mother died, her dad stopped attending and the subject faded away. Sunday mornings were spent resting at home or grocery shopping. Valarie remembered the good sensation she felt after going to church and being with fellow believers. There was a sense of peace and friendship in the building, the feeling she couldn't get anywhere else. Her family enjoyed it, even though her dad always said that he only went because his wife wanted him to.

All day that Sunday Valarie tried to push her anxious thoughts away and to occupy her mind. Then she realized that she had already been doing that, so she tried not to think about what she was afraid of or what could go wrong, and she realized she had already tried that too. So instead she tried the two efforts again while she did her laundry. I'm the boss, she told herself. I'm in charge. That night as she lay in bed, she waited to see if the anxiety would come. The troublesome thoughts came the moment her head hit the pillow, so she picked up a fiction book and started to read. She paused every so often to tell herself, "I'm the boss." She read for about an hour before she began to feel sleepy. Finally she set her book on the nightstand, turned off her light and closed her eyes to go to sleep.

The next night after her father went to bed, Valarie stayed in her day clothes and went outside. She walked the orchard, looking for any sign of David. Tiny met her first, and Valarie knelt down to pet the dog. David soon caught up and aimed his flashlight at the ground. Valarie stood and gave David a warm smile. David was silent, as if he was waiting to hear how she was feeling. She shrugged her shoulders. "I walked out of my house this time," she said, feeling rather happy. David smiled a smile that she had never seen before. His eyes were soft yet they sparkled, and Valarie could make out a red color on his cheeks. *Was he blushing?* she wondered. *Was it something I said?* She had never seen him blush before. She thought his red face looked adorable, and she smiled back at him.

"That's good," David said. "It's nice to see you on your feet instead of on your hands and knees."

Valarie felt her own face grow hot. "It feels nice too."

The days began to pass and Valarie's panic runs to the orchard were becoming less and less. Even though she still struggled with her thoughts and nervousness, David said it would take time to work through it completely, and Valarie felt all right to give it time. The two began to meet each other in the orchard at night and walk the property with Tiny or sit on his front porch for a late night snack. During the day Valarie saw David in English class, but the two didn't have a chance to talk until lunchtime when David would come to sit with her. She began to expect him wherever she went and soon she didn't mind his company, even though she still thought he was a little weird. Between lunch and their nightly meetings, the two had talked about every subject they could think of: English, the founding fathers, animals, even cars and video games. David had offered for her to come over to play his racing game, but Valarie told him some other time. She was embarrassed to tell him that she didn't know how to play any video games. She talked about some of her favorite fictional books, and he told her about his love of art. He promised to show Valarie his art sometime in the near future.

The two planned a weekly tutoring session with her dad, and David said his grades were actually improving for the first time in his three years of high school. He had told her dad that he really needed the good grades to get into a good college after graduation from high school that spring. Valarie didn't want to think about what would happen to her after he graduated. She knew with him gone, she would go back to being alone all the time, and she didn't want to think about that. As she stood in the bathroom one night, brushing her teeth, she looked in the mirror and paused. She stared at herself, wondering what it was about her appearance that looked so different. Then she realized it was her entire being. For the first time in perhaps her whole life, she saw a happy face looking back at her, even though she still had stress lines and tired eyes. Her face seemed to glow and whenever she thought of David, she smiled. No one had ever made her smile just by thinking of them. David was making a difference in her life, and it showed on the outside. Suddenly her lungs felt tight. She knew she liked him, maybe as much as he liked her, but she didn't want to admit it. She couldn't. She was too awkward and shy. He'd already come to like her despite her flaws, why couldn't she accept that? Inside she felt too broken and too messed up for anyone to like her. Yet on the outside, a nice boy was talking to her and smiling at her almost every day, twice a day even. David cared for her. He was helping her through issues he himself had overcome. She felt as ease around him, and almost felt sad whenever she had to leave him for the night. Having a good friend like him was almost too good to be true. For the first time since freshman year, she had met someone whom she didn't want to leave her alone.

David had finished his lunch in his usual ten minutes while Valarie took her time to eat as always. She had once asked David why he ate so fast, but he just shrugged and gulped down his full soda can.

"So," he said, wiping his mouth with his still folded napkin. "We seniors are having a spring formal this weekend. Of course you wouldn't know anything about it since you're a junior," he playfully nudged her with his elbow.

"Compared to a senior citizen," she teased back.

David was silent for a moment, then he said, "I get to bring someone with me…and…I was wondering if…you'd like to go with me."

Valarie slowly set down her fork. *Did he just ask me to a school dance?* The voice rang out in her head. She had spent three years of high school all by herself, no friend, no date for a dance, she hadn't even attended a dance, and much less any school function that wasn't required and here was David, asking her to go with him to his senior spring formal. Suddenly her stomach gave a churn.

"Has nobody asked you to go with them?" she said, hoping he wasn't asking her as his only option.

"Well, yeah someone did," he stuttered. "But, I wanted to ask you."

Valarie's heart began to beat faster, and her lungs grew tight. She wasn't his last option, she was his first. She knew he liked her, but she didn't know he liked her enough to turn down someone else, unless the other girl was flat out ugly.

"Umm…" she said, trying to get enough oxygen back to her brain to answer. "I don't usually go to those things."

"Ever?"

Valarie shook her head.

"Well, there's a first time for everything," he said. He laid his hand down on the table and tapped his fingers. Then he moved his hand closer as if he was trying to build up the courage to take her hand. Valarie clasped her hands together and set them on her lap. She didn't want to be rude to him, but she didn't want to hold his hand.

"I'd really like it if you'd come with me," he continued. His voice was honest, but not pleading.

Valarie tried to swallow the lump in her throat. "I… don't know. I think I have something planned with my dad that day," she said, hoping that her father actually would have something for her to do so that she wouldn't have to go. In the past, she never had any reason to go to a school dance. She didn't have any friends to go with and no one had ever invited her. Now David was asking her to go as his date. The thought scared her. She didn't want to be in a crowd of kids who ignored her every day with the only person who didn't. The thought was frightening.

David nodded. "All right. Will you let me know if you're free?"

Valarie stood to her feet and grabbed her lunch tray. "Yeah, sure. I'm late. I'll see you later."

Once again she walked away from him, feeling self-conscious and mystified as to why she was still running away.

"You've been quiet, Val. Are you feeling okay?"

Valarie looked up from her dinner plate, not feeling hungry enough to eat her fish. "Yeah, I'm okay."

"Uh oh, you've got your 'I'm having a dilemma' voice. What's going on?"

Valarie wished her father didn't know her well enough to tell when she was having trouble with something. Then again, she wanted to tell somebody.

"Someone's asked me the senior dance," she said, knowing that she might be signing David's death certificate.

"I see," her dad said. "And what did you tell David?"

How did he know? she asked herself. Then again, who else would it have been? "I told him I might have plans."

"What day is this dance?" He seemed to be taking it lightly.

"This Saturday."

Tom stared off into space, as if he was thinking. "No. I think we're free. Why don't you go?"

Because the guy likes me and I'm afraid of being liked and also afraid of liking him and him wanting some kind of relationship, she wanted to say. She almost wished her dad was forbidding her to go.

"I don't have anything to wear," she said.

Her dad set his fork down on his plate, making a clink sound echo through the otherwise empty dining room. "Well, if you want to go we can find you something to wear. I don't want you to stay home just because you don't have something appropriate to wear."

What about because I'm scared? she thought. It sounded like a good enough excuse to herself.

After school the next day, her dad had taken her around town to all the second hand and thrift stores in search of a decent dress. After a few horrific options of an ugly green tank top and a velvet dress from her dad, she could tell he didn't really know what to do in this case, so she told him she would just look around and hope that he wouldn't suggest any more clothes from his century. She didn't see anything she liked, nor did she want to be picking out something she knew David might say she looked pretty in. She didn't see herself as pretty, and was afraid of anyone telling her otherwise.

"What about this?" her dad asked, holding a flower printed dress that reached down to the floor.

"It's too long," Valarie said.

"That's why I'm suggesting it." He wore a sort of proud look on his face.

Valarie laughed. An hour later she still hadn't found something of her taste. She had tried on fifteen dresses in all the thrift shops in town, and nothing pleased her.

"It's all right, Dad, I'll just pick something from my closet."

Her father glanced at something in the distance, and a light bulb seemed to turn on over his head. "The closet!" he cried. "Why didn't I think of that before?" He took his daughter's hand and rushed out to his truck. He drove home like a mad man, smiling and telling himself how much of a genius he was. Valarie was wondering if he was having some sort of breakdown. Once they got home, he told Valarie to stay in the living room while he rushed up stairs. Valarie was growing worried. Within a few minutes he came back with a dress that hung on a blue padded hanger. He held it up in front of himself for Valarie to see. A V neck black dress with large elegant red roses printed along the bottom half from the torso down. It wasn't too short, or too long, and the straps were tank top width. It was perfect.

She smiled then frowned as she had the sensation that she had seen it before.

"Yes, it was your mother's," her dad said, as if he was answering her silent question. "She only wore it on special occasion, manly Christmas Eve services."

Valarie gently touched the soft cotton fabric. She could remember seeing her mother wearing the dress as she stood in the candlelit church singing carols with her beautiful voice.

"Dad...I can't," she said, suddenly forcing away tears.

"Yes, you can, and you will," her dad said gently. "I think it'll fit you." He held up to her for measurement.

"It was Mom's," she said. She felt a tear slip out of her eye and down her cheek.

"I know. And she would want you to have something beautiful to wear for your first school dance." He wiped the tear off her cheek, and Valarie could see that he was fighting back tears himself. "I only wish she was here. She could help you more than I could. I don't know how to curl hair or put on makeup."

Valarie giggled through her tears. "It's all right. I'll figure it out." She took the dress and admired it some more. She didn't realize her dad had stepped out of the room until he came back from upstairs and handed her a pair of red pumps. "She always wore these with the dress."

Valarie nodded. She remembered exactly how her mother looked last year, and she wanted to look just like her. "Thanks, Dad." Her father hugged her tightly, making the moment even mushier then it already was. He suddenly pulled away and announced that he was going to make dinner. Valarie went up to her room and hung the dress over her door mirror. She left it there until later that night when she went to bed. She changed into her pajamas and sat on her bed for a while, staring at the dress. She thought of her mother's bright smiled and long brown curls that bounced on her shoulders. Her mother was so pretty, with a face that many women told her looked so innocent and young. A thought ran through Valarie's head, and she resisted the urge to run. Instead she felt a tear roll down her face and she quickly wiped it away. She turned out her lamp and lay down, trying to avoid wondering why her mother had to die.

Valarie went to school the next day and deliberately searched for David. She wanted to tell him that she would go with him to the dance now that she had something appropriate to wear. She spotted him outside the door of English class, talking to Eric and waiting for the teacher to show up. They both turned when she approached him.

"Hey, Valarie," David said, his face brightened.

She opened her mouth to speak, but the words wouldn't come.

"Are you all right?" he asked.

Just do it, she told herself, *do it!* "I'm going," she blurted out.

"Going where?" David dragged out the words.

Way to break it, she scolded herself. "I mean," she corrected herself, shaking her head. "I'll go. With you. To the dance. If you still want me to." She could feel Eric watching her make a fool of herself, but she didn't care. The smile on David's face when she told him was enough to make her rob a bank just to see it again.

CHAPTER 6

Breathe, Valarie, breathe. I can't breathe! the voice in her head screamed.

Valarie stood in front of the mirror in her bedroom observing her reflection. Her dad had rushed her home from school that day and insisted that she spend the rest of the evening pampering herself for her big night. After her shower, he gave her some of her mother's makeup to wear and after an hour's worth of watching online tutorials, she began to apply the makeup, hoping she wouldn't poke her eye out. Her dad also gave her a bottle of her mother's perfume, the one Valarie found the most comforting. After drying her hair, she asked to borrow her mother's curling iron and spent the next hour producing curls. *No wonder I don't do this every day*, she thought, *it's too much work*. She slipped on the dress and her heart dropped. The V cut shape almost made her feel too exposed, even though she knew she wasn't showing anything. She had never worn anything so elegant and pretty before, she almost felt like she was in someone else's skin.

"It's all right," she said aloud then went over to her bed to sit and put on the shoes. She never realized that she was the same size as her mother until now. She could remember herself as mama's little girl when she was really mama's young woman.

David had said he'd pick her up in his dad's car around six thirty. Valarie glanced at the clock on her night stand. It was twenty after six. She gasped for air.

"It's all right," she told herself. "It's just a dance. I'll be okay. I got this." She felt like she was choking underneath the perfume and face paint. She went back to the mirror, careful to make sure that she looked perfect.

A knock came at her door, and she almost jumped out of the dress. *He can't be here yet!* she thought. "Come in," she said, her voice trembling.

The door slowly squeaked open and her dad poked his face in. A look of surprise and astonishment came across his face. "Wow," he said, opening the door fully and stepping in to her room. "You look so much like your mom. I would have guessed you were her." He seemed to be transfixed in a memory.

"Do I look all right?" she asked, the nervousness in her voice was unmistakable.

Her dad nodded.

Valarie noticed that he was fighting back tears.

"Why are you crying?" she asked, thinking that she had done something wrong.

"I wish she was here to see this." Her dad sniffed.

"Don't cry. If you cry, I'll start crying and the makeup I spent forty minutes trying to put on will start to run."

Her dad laughed and wiped his tears. He approached Valarie and held her close. "You've grown up so fast, daughter," he said with a sigh. "Only yesterday you were taking off your diaper wanting to run around the house naked." They stood in each other's arms until a knock came at the door downstairs. Her heart jumped into her throat. She knew it was too late to back out now.

Her dad let go of her and smiled. "You come out whenever you're ready," he said gently then left to answer the door.

I don't think I'll ever be ready, she thought. She looked herself over in the mirror one more time. *Okay, here goes nothing*. She held her breath and she emerged from the bedroom, almost tripping over her own feet in the heels. She slowly walked down the hallway and entered the living room. David's back was turned to her, but he turned around when he saw her dad look behind him and smile. David's eyes wandered from her head, to her shoes, then her head again.

"Wow," he said, as if he couldn't find any other words. "You look amazing, Valarie."

Valarie's face grew hot. "Thanks," she croaked. She noticed his appearance. He didn't wear a traditional tux, but his hair was combed back and he wore a deep blue long sleeve shirt and black dress pants. *He looks so fine*, she thought to herself. "You look great too," she said, remembering to return the compliment. Valarie saw his face turn red, and he tried to hide a nervous smile. Her heart fluttered at the sight of his bashful face. It was still so cute.

"Is anybody going to comment on how I look?" Tom asked. David turned to face him and Valarie laughed.

"You look very…collected, sir," David said.

Her dad waved his hand. "All right. Now, stand together, I want a picture."

David stepped close enough to Valarie that she could smell his cologne. It smelled very pleasant to her. She smiled for the camera then smiled again when David asked Tom to take a picture on his smartphone. It took him a few minutes as he tried to figure out how the dang thing worked. Once he finally snapped the picture he gave the phone back and waved his hand. "All right, you two, have a good time."

Valarie hugged her dad one last time. "Thanks for everything," she whispered. She let go of him, feeling like she let go of the little girl she had been since her mom passed. The two walked out to David's car. He opened the door for her then got in on the driver's side. "You ready?" he asked. His face was red even in the setting sun.

Valarie nodded and David drove them to the school. "I got to be honest, Val, you look amazing," he said, once they pulled out onto the highway.

Valarie smiled. "I feel really silly," she confessed.

"Don't. You look beautiful."

There they were, the words she had been afraid to hear since the day he asked her to go to the dance with him. He found her beautiful, he saw her beautiful. *Did he see me that way without the dress and makeup?* she wondered. She wanted to believe he did, yet at the same time, she didn't want to believe it at all. "Thanks."

David reached over the middle seat and took Valarie's hand. She felt the same electricity surge through her arm just as she had the day they met and shook hands.

"I know this is all new for you, but I just want you to know that I'm grateful that you decided to come with me. And don't worry; I'll have you home by eleven."

"Okay," she said. It was all Valarie could think of saying. Her mind was very aware of the feeling of his hand in hers. She wanted to pull away from him, but at the same time, she liked holding his hand. It was all too new and exciting for someone who'd never held a hand or was told they were beautiful by anyone other than a parent. She suddenly felt very sheltered and was glad she agreed to go with him.

The two tried to fill the car ride with simple conversation, but it seemed that neither of them could find anything fascinating to talk about for very long. When they got to the school, David pulled into a spot farthest from the entrance and turned off the car. He got out then he hurried over to the passenger door to open it for Valarie before she could let herself out. He took her hand and began to walk toward the gym. Valarie felt a sense of pride and excitement walking hand in hand with someone who liked her enough to invite her to a formal gathering. It made her feel grown up and worry free, something she had never felt in her life. She looked up from their hands and saw the sunset. Colors of pink and red were mixed in with sky blue and yellows. They spread across the sky like a brushstroke. She smiled. David followed her gaze.

"It's beautiful, huh?" he asked.

Valarie nodded. Suddenly David stopped in his tracks and shoved his hand in his pocket. "I almost forgot," he said. He pulled out a silver chain with a small charm on it. The charm was a silver interwoven cross with a red ruby in the center.

"For me?" she asked, looking up at him.

"Of course. Who else would it be for?" he asked with his dazzling smile. He walked behind her and reached over her shoulders to fasten the necklace around her neck. Valarie moved all her curls to the right side of her shoulder to give him enough room to fasten the chain.

"It's beautiful, David. Thank you."

He faced her again, with a hint of red on his checks. "You're very welcome. I'm glad you like it."

"I love it," she said with a smile.

He took her hand again and they continued to the gym. As they passed through the entryway, a tall blue flower covered arch stood a few feet away before the door. A photographer was kneeling down with a large camera, taking pictures of all the kids entering the dance. When it came time for Valarie and David, she felt him slip his arm around her waist and pull her close to his side. She tried not to get anxious about his arm where it was long enough to smile for the picture. Once the flash came and went, David let go of her, took her hand once again, and continued on into the gym without so much as a word. Inside the gym, Valarie was overtaken by her surroundings. The lights were off, yet spot lights in a variety of colors shown down everywhere. Blue and red streamers hung from the walls. A long table with food and drink sat up against the right wall, decorated with long blue table cloths and red roses. Valarie noticed the red and blue theme. She looked down at her dress with the red roses then she looked at David in his blue shirt.

"We match," he said, over the blaring loud music. It was just what Valarie was thinking. She smiled. She was still trying to get over the feeling of his arm around her. Then a thought struck her. Would he want to dance with her? *Of course, stupid*, she told herself, *that's why he invited you. You obviously haven't thought this through*. He led her over to the drink table and poured her a cup of punch. She drank it slowly before he led her out onto the dance floor. The song was a fast paced one, and once he got into the crowd he started to move his body freely. Valarie stood frozen in the spot.

David stopped. "What's wrong?" he asked.

"I don't know how to dance," she shouted over the music.

A smile came to David's face. He took her hands and held her gaze. He swayed to the left then to the right. Valarie followed his movement. He stepped back, still holding her hands. She stepped forward then stepped back as he had. *I'm dancing!* she thought. She laughed aloud. He twirled her under his arm then he pulled her close to him as he had done moments before. He held one hand with hers, and slid the other behind her, still moving to the music. Valarie wanted to push him away and run out of the gym, but she tried to remain calm. *It's all right, you're just dancing,* she told herself. She tried to move along with him, but she found it a little difficult to keep up. When the song ended she was a little disappointed, and she was glad when David kept dancing into the next one. After three songs she was feeling a little out of breath. David must have noticed, for he took her hand and lead her out of the crowd to the side.

"Are you all right?" he asked.

Valarie nodded. She needed some clear air. "I'm going to go the girl's room."

David walked her out of the gym. The air in the halls wasn't so stuffy, and it felt cool to her hot face. She went into the bathroom and checked herself in the mirror. Her face was flushed. She grabbed a handful of paper towels, wet them and held it to her face. It felt good. She was about to splash water on her face when a group of girls came into the bathroom, chatting and laughing together. Two went into the stalls while the other approached the sink and began to fix her makeup. Valarie saw her look at her with surprise.

"Hey," the girl said to her, looking at her in the mirror. Then she turned to Valarie and asked, "Your David's girlfriend, right?"

"Um, well, I wouldn't call us boyfriend and girlfriend," she answered.

The girl smiled. She was pretty with long blonde hair and brown eyes that were brought out by her grey makeup. "I would. He always talks about you." She must have seen the confused look on Valarie's face, for she said. "I'm Emma. David and I are lab partners in chemistry class."

"Oh," Valarie said, not knowing what else to say.

"He talks about you all the time. He really likes you, you know." She began to apply some lip gloss.

Valarie waited for the girl to start laughing at the joke she must have been playing, but the girl was sincere.

"Really?" Valarie asked, now absorbed in what she was being told.

"Yeah. I had even asked him to come to the dance, but he said he had already asked someone else, I guess that was you." The girl smiled kindly. "You're a lucky girl, Valarie."

The other two girls came near the sink and they all patched up their makeup before leaving the bathroom. Valarie stood there for a few moments trying to take it all in. She knew David liked her, but just how much did he like her, enough to want to be boyfriend and girlfriend? Valarie didn't even know how a relationship worked. She had never had a boyfriend before or even thought of having one. She suddenly wondered what she had gotten herself into. She didn't want to leave David wondering why she couldn't have a relationship with him, but she didn't want to jump in without a clue as to how it worked. Maybe she could learn? Maybe she could take it slow? She suddenly realized that she liked being with him enough to try a relationship.

She walked out of the bathroom to find David waiting for her down the hall. He turned toward her and smiled. "Feel better?" he asked.

"My feet hurt a bit," she confessed.

"Would you like to sit for a minute?" he asked, taking her hand.

"That would be nice."

The two went back into the gym and she wondered exactly what David had said about her in class, or to anyone else for that matter. She hoped it was all good things and nothing personal. She felt that David wouldn't betray her trust that way. He stopped near the wall and offered for Valarie to take a seat. Her feet began to feel relieved.

"I'll let you rest for a moment while I go over there and say hi to some friends. Is that okay?"

Valarie nodded. She watched David go, almost sorry that her feet hurt too much to go with him. She sat and listened to the music for a while before someone approached her. She thought it was David, but when she looked up, she saw it was Eric.

"Wow," he said, observing her appearance. "You clean up good."

Valarie didn't know whether to feel insulted or flattered.

"Where's your date?" he asked, standing next to the chair beside her.

"He went to say hello to a friend."

"So, he's got you talking and to going out with him in just a few weeks, huh?"

Valarie now felt insulted. "Is that a problem?" she asked. She didn't care that she sounded hostile.

"No, especially if it gets you looking like this," he sat down next to her. "You want to go get something to drink?" he asked. Valarie could feel his eyes travel all over her. She swallowed hard. "No," she said plainly.

Suddenly someone cleared their throat loud enough to be heard over the music. The two turned and saw David standing behind her. He looked thoroughly offended at Eric. He placed his hand on Valarie's shoulder as if to let her know that he would protect her. Eric stood to his feet and looked embarrassed. "Hey, how's it going?" he asked David.

"It's going," David said. His face was lifeless as he glared at Eric.

"All right, see you around." Eric began to walk away. Valarie jumped when David suddenly took his arm. "Not cool," she heard him say. Then he let go of Eric and let him walk away.

David sat in the seat on the other side of Valarie. "Are you okay?" he asked sincerely.

Valarie nodded. She knew that she would be safe with David, as if he was her knight in shining armor.

"You want to dance some more?" David asked.

"Yeah," she answered. They danced for a few minutes before a slow song came on. David took her hand and pulled her close with the other, just like he had done earlier. "Is this all right?" he asked.

Valarie nodded. She could feel his hand on her waist as if it was burning through her. She cautiously placed her left hand on his shoulder, and let him lead. On an impulse, she leaned her head on his chest, and could hear the thumping of his heart. Even though she didn't know the song, David did, and she could hear the vibrations in his airways as he hummed along. Even though she was scared, Valarie enjoyed being held. She wondered if David was enjoying himself too. She spotted the girl she had seen in the bathroom earlier, standing off to the wall. The girl saw her too, for she gave Valarie two thumbs up. Valarie smiled then closed her eyes to take in the moment. He held her close for what felt like forever, but when the song ended, it ended all too soon. She didn't want the moment to end.

CHAPTER 7

The night air felt cool to Valarie's skin as soon as it touched her face. The dance hadn't ended yet, but the two had danced all they could for one night. Valarie's feet were killing her. She slipped the heels off once she got inside the car and she could feel the first signs of a headache coming on. She was glad to get out of the crowded gym, but she didn't want to go home just yet.

David seemed to know where he was driving and soon he parked the car in an empty parking lot not too far from the school.

"Where are we?" Valarie asked.

"The park," David said, taking off his seatbelt. "I thought we could take a walk in the night air, unless you're ready to go home."

Valarie shook her head. "No this is fine," she said, unbuckling herself as well. David opened her door again, and she swung her feet out of the car. She hesitated, dreading the thought of having to put the heels back on her aching feet.

"Hang on," David said, going around to the back of the car. He opened the trunk and rummaged through it for a moment before slamming it shut and walking back over to her. "My mom always carries an extra pair of shoes for herself whenever she gets tired of her heels. I think these might fit you." He held out a pair of brown leather sandals.

"Thanks." Valarie smiled and put them on.

"Perfect," David said, seeing that they fit. He took her hand and the two took a slow walk through the grass toward the playground.

A small breeze swept through Valarie's hair, cooling her ears and neck. She didn't know what she wanted more, to get out of her dress and wash all the makeup off, or to spend more time with David. She knew her curfew was coming up, and she didn't want to rush the rest of the night away. She wanted to enjoy every moment she had of being with him.

They approached the swing set and Valarie seated herself on a swing that felt like it would give way any second. David went behind her and gave her a small push on the chains that held the swing to the iron bars overhead. They squeaked.

"Are you having a good time?" he asked her.

"I am."

"Good. I'm really glad you decided to come with me." He gave her one more push then he sat on the swing next to her. He stared at her with an inexpressible gaze, as if he was looking past her into space.

"What?" she asked, wondering what he was thinking.

He shook his head. "Nothing. I just can't get over how beautiful you look."

Valarie felt her face grow hot. She looked away from David and picked at a piece of lint on her dress. "What about without the makeup and hair?"

"What about it?"

"Do you find me pretty even then?"

"I do," he said. "I've found you pretty since the day I met you, when you were wearing a red T shirt with a brown coat and blue jeans."

She looked at him in surprise. "You remember what I was wearing?"

"Sure do. You looked like a rustic country girl." He smiled.

"I am a country girl," she said matter-of-factly. "I never dress up, except for special occasions."

"That's not a bad thing. Too much face paint and you'll look like an ape threw a paint ball at you."

Valarie laughed.

"You have a nice laugh," David said, his voice starting to sound dreamy. He rose to his feet and stood in front of her. He took her hand and gently pulled her to her feet.

Very slowly, he slipped his arms around her and began to lean close to her. Valarie saw him close his eyes as she felt his strong arms tighten. She knew he was going to kiss her. *Oh no*, she thought. She gently pushed him away then took a small step back. Her chest began to feel tight, like she was suffocating.

David opened his eyes. He looked confused. "Is something wrong?"

"No...don't," she said, pushing him away and getting out of his embrace.

"Valarie, what's wrong?"

"I have to go," she said. She pushed past David and began walking. She didn't know where she was going, she just wanted to get away from him.

"What's wrong?" David asked again. He started to follow her.

Valarie didn't answer him, she just kept walking. She could feel his presence when he caught up with her.

"Did I do something wrong?"

She shook her head. She tasted something salty on her lips and realized that she had started crying.

"Valarie, talk to me," David said gently, taking her hand. "Please, tell me what's wrong."

"You can't do this." She cried.

"Do what?"

"This, all this." She waved her hands around in the air, as if she was a bird trying to take flight. "You can't be nice to me, you can't like me, you can't try to kiss me." She pulled her hand away from him and continued walking, faster this time.

"Why not?" he asked, struggling to keep up with her pace.

Valarie was silent. Suddenly her head began to throb and she felt a longing to go home.

"Why not?" he asked again, a little louder than before.

Valarie shook her head again. *Don't ask me*, she screamed at him in her mind, *I can't tell you. I don't want to tell you.*

"Valarie!" He took her by the arm. She yanked it away.

"Because!" Valarie shouted. David stopped abruptly. He had never heard Valarie shout before. She stood still, staring at him with tears spilling out of her eyes. "Because you can't be with me. I'm not…I'm not…" She didn't know what else to say. *I'm not lovable? I'm not normal?* What reason was good enough to make him leave her alone? "I'm too messed up for someone like you."

David blinked. "I don't see you that way," he said calmly.

"I am!" she cried. "I can't be with anyone with all the flaws and fears that I have."

"Valarie, you're fine. You've been working through your fears," he said. His eyebrows pulled together with a look of sympathy.

"You don't understand," she said. "I don't want anyone to love me."

David slowly approached her. "Why not?"

She took in a deep breath and wiped her face. *Don't say it*, she told herself, *you've already messed up the evening with your stupid fear.* "Because I don't know how," she said, almost choking over the words. "Because I can't deal with my problem and try to be with someone at the same time. I don't want to lose anyone else." She didn't mean to give him so many reasons. They all just came spilling out when she opened her big mouth.

David looked confused still. "Valarie, you've been doing great with your anxiety. I've seen some real progress in you."

She shook her head. "I don't feel better, David. Sometimes I am so full of stress and anxieties that I just want to hit somebody, or scream, or go to sleep and never wake up. Sometimes I don't even want to live to see another day if that means I'm going to suffer all over again."

David looked down at his feet as if he was thinking. *Now you've done it,* she told herself, *you confessed something so deep and scared away the first friend you've had in nine years.* She was surprised when David slowly approached her and cautiously took her hand.

"Come on," he said in a soft voice.

"Where are we going?" she asked. She suddenly felt exhausted.

"Someplace that will make you feel better," he said. He began to lead her to his car. "Don't take me to the hospital," she pleaded.

David stopped and turned to her. "Why would I take you to the hospital?" A different type of confusion was spread across his face.

"Because I just told you I don't want to live through the anxiety?" she said. *Is that not a good enough reason?* she asked herself.

David almost smiled. "Valarie, hospitals are for sick people, and crazy people. You're neither one. You just have some emotions that you need to work through."

She hesitated before confessing, "I don't know how." Her voice was so quiet it was almost a whisper.

"I know," he said, placing his other hand over hers that he already held. She could feel it trembling in his grasp. "I'm going to help you."

CHAPTER 8

David sat across from Valarie in the tiny booth of the local diner. He had driven her to a small hole in the wall called Ian's, and sat her down while he went to order "something that will fix everything." A few minutes later he came back with two old-fashioned hamburgers and two chocolate milkshakes.

"Here we go," he said. "Just what you need."

"How is this supposed to fix anything?" she asked, almost feeling annoyed that he was thinking of something to eat while she was crying.

"Well, for starters, it'll help your stomach to get some food, and while you eat, we're going to work out what it is that's making you feel like you've been drowning on the inside."

Here it was, a chance to talk about everything that had been hurting her, everything that made her worried and scared, and she didn't want it. She wanted to go home, to pull the covers over her head and sleep for a few days. She felt exhausted. She almost wished David wasn't so caring, that way she could have been spared the agony of letting out all the emotion she held inside.

"Whenever you're ready to talk, I'm all ears," David said, taking a bite of his burger.

Valarie took a deep breath. She knew he wasn't going to leave it alone. *You might as well as talk*, she told herself. *It's about time someone lent an ear to you.*

"I've always been a shy and quiet kid," she began, "Never really outgoing, always hiding behind mommy's leg or in daddy's arms. I'll be the first to admit I'm rather sheltered. My parents tried to get me involved in activities and friendships, but I never wanted them. I didn't want change in my life. Everything they enrolled me in I dropped out of. All the slumber parties I went to I would break down and start crying to the point where the friend's parent would call my mom to come get me because I was 'upsetting the other kids.' Soon my parents stopped trying to push me out of the nest, and all the people I knew didn't want to hang around with me anymore, because I was no fun."

She choked back the tears as she came to the hard part of her story. "Then my mother got sick. She was sick for a long time, and it was one hospital and doctor visit after another. She was getting better, or so she said she was, and for a while she stopped getting treatment. The hospital bills were piling up and she was afraid that she would put my dad and I in debt. So she tried to take care of herself as best as she could. One day she collapsed in the kitchen and Dad rushes her to the ER. They give her one round of treatment, hoping it will sustain her for a little while, but they knew she wouldn't make it. She spent three weeks in the hospital, losing her hair and vomiting up everything she tried to take in because the medicine messed with her stomach. All sorts of tubes were stuck in her arms and hands. I couldn't even hold her hand because she had so many needles in them. She was so sick. I had never seen anyone that sick."

Valarie turned and looked out the window. She saw her reflection and noticed that her makeup was running, but she didn't care to wipe it away.

"The day she died," she continued, "I asked my dad if I could take the day off school and spend it with her. I knew she wasn't going to last long. I think he did too, and that's why he agreed to let me go. I spent a few hours at the hospital with her, trying to make her smile and get her mind off the pain, but her stomach was sick most of that day, and my dad eventually just took me home. That night…" she paused.

She could still hear the sound of her dad's cell phone ringing, and how many times it rung before he woke enough to answer the call. She knew it was the hospital. She knew her mother was gone.

"He didn't even get to say good-bye. Neither of us did. And then the holidays came, and they just seemed to feel empty without her." She picked up a napkin and wiped her eyes. David sat in silence, listening to her pour her heart out. "Ever since then, I pretty much shut everyone out, and became afraid of suffering as much as she did. I didn't care that I was quiet, and that nobody liked me. I was better off by myself anyway. I did what I could to manage my anxiety and fear. I'll admit it wasn't enough, and I was beginning to think that I would take it to my grave."

She looked up at him and noticed that he had tears in his eyes. "And then, one day, this kid comes along. And… he shows me what it's like to be worry free, and not have to wonder about what fear might come true that day. He helps me and supports me, and I have nothing for him, nothing but fear of opening up to him. I never thought someone like you would come along, David. And now that you have, I'm scared. I don't know how to be in a relationship, I don't know what I am to give you in return. I can't even be near you without freaking out about what I'm supposed to say or do. I don't know how to love anyone."

David looked down at the plate he had abandoned once she started talking. He folded his hand and rested his chin on them. He seemed to be thinking. Valarie wondered if he was going to tell her that they shouldn't be friends anymore, that she really was too emotional for him to handle. Her stomach churned from fear that he now hated her.

"Valarie," he said, his voice quivering. "I'm sorry you had to watch someone you love suffer. And I'm sorry that you didn't get the chance to say good-bye. I know it's a heavy load to carry." He placed his hand on the table palm facing up. Valarie hesitated yet she placed her hand in his. "But I want you to know, that I don't see you as messed up or too broken to love. Who said we had to love each other right now anyway?"

Valarie looked confused. "You tried to kiss me at the park," she explained.

"Yeah," he said, "but I don't think I love you, not yet anyway. I mean, I really like you, a lot, but I know that we're still just two kids trying to get through high school. Besides, nobody knows how a relationship works at first. They have to learn how it works. We're not born knowing everything, unfortunately."

Valarie felt stupid. She had expected too much from David assuming that he felt more than she did, all because she was afraid that he might have felt differently for her.

"Val," he said, giving her hand a gentle squeeze. "I don't care that you're shy and reserved. It's a character trait you grew up with, and will more than likely have for the rest of your life. But, like I've been telling you when we talk about your anxiety, you can't let it box you in and keep you from the life you're meant to live."

"What life is that, David? I don't have anyone or anything to offer."

"Sure you do," he said. "You have numerous talents and abilities and dreams to work at. Don't tell me there's not one thing in this world that you'd like to do?"

Valarie thought for a moment. *What is something I'd like to do with my life?* she asked herself. "I want to go to college."

"Well, there you go. You have a dream to further your education. And it'll be one of the best choices you ever made."

"I can't even get through the day in a high school, how am I supposed to get into college?" she asked with a tone of disbelief.

"You're a junior, aren't you?"

"Yeah."

"Well, you've gone through more than a day. You've gone through three whole years, which equals out to…" he stopped to think for a moment. "One thousand and ninety-five days of high school, so far."

Valarie stared at David. What was he trying to get at?

"Valarie, I know you're scared, but I don't want anything from you that you're not ready or willing to give. You don't want to be with me than just say so. Don't worry about hurting my feelings, they'll grow back, I'm like a starfish."

Valarie giggled through her tears.

"You don't need to be afraid to open up to someone. You've been holding this in for so long that it's keeping you from something as simple as having a friend. It's okay to let it go; you need to let it go. I can see how much it's eating at you."

"I don't have anyone to talk to," she said.

"You have me," he corrected. "We've been talking for over a month now."

"But who will I have when you leave?"

"Where am I going?" he asked, his eyes growing wide.

"Aren't you going to college after your graduation this summer?"

David smiled and threw his head back. "Oh, Val," he said with a sigh. "You assume way too much for what reality actually holds." He faced her, and Valarie could see the sparkle in his eyes. "I don't think I'll go anywhere after I graduate."

"What about furthering your education?"

"Well, that's where something called online school comes in. I have a good life here, I have a few friends, and I have you."

"Don't stay behind for me. Don't let me hold you back like that." She started to sob again.

"I'm not, Valarie. Truth is, I didn't get in anywhere I wanted. So, I'll take the alternative and study online. It's not what I want, but it will give me a degree that will get me good job. Maybe going off to college wasn't meant to be. Maybe I'm supposed to stay here."

Valarie sighed. She had assumed two things about David before she even asked him how he felt or what his plans were. If this wasn't evidence of being messed up, she didn't know what was.

"We don't have to worry about anything if we don't want to. We're still kids. All we need to do is take one day at a time. Don't worry about the future or what we can't change. That's all useless worrying that will stress you out. And stress isn't cool." He leaned over the table and wiped the tears from her face. "I'm sorry if I offended you. I didn't mean to. We were just having such a good night and...I guess I got carried away."

"And I've ruined it," Valarie said, waving at her tear-stained face as evidence.

"Nah," David said, shifting in his seat. "You needed to let it out. You needed closure, and I'm just glad I was here for you."

Valarie smiled as best she could. She felt like a real mess, but at the same time, she felt better. She had let out all her emotions and anger to someone who cared and listened. David had seen her, the real her. And he was sitting across from her waiting for her to empty her heart out so he could take it and patch it up.

"Sometimes I wonder why you came into my life," she said. Her voice was so quiet it was almost a whisper.

"Because God knew you needed someone your age that's already been through this, to help you." The tears started to come back into his eyes.

Valarie looked up at the ceiling and breathed in deep. This God he was always talking about sure had a funny way of carrying out things.

"I'm sorry I assumed so much," she said, still looking up.

"Don't worry about it. You were concerned. That tells me you like me."

She looked down at him and saw the clever smile on his face. She giggled.

"And about the kiss, I'm sorry. I shouldn't have done that. I promise I will only kiss you if you want to be kissed."

Valarie looked down at the table. She had forgotten about the food he ordered for her. It was probably cold. "What do we do now?" she asked.

David sighed. "First we're eating this food before it gets any colder. Second, I got to take you home so your dad doesn't shoot me for bringing you back late, and third, you're going to get a good night's sleep, and we're going to try again tomorrow. That's all we can do right now."

Valarie nodded. "I'm sorry," she said, feeling silly for breaking down in front of the poor boy on a night that was supposed to be fun and exciting.

David shook his head. "Don't be sorry. You've been strong for a while now, and you just needed a break."

She wiped her face again. She didn't realize that she was thirsty until she caught sight of her chocolate shake. She took a big long sip. It was delicious and cool on her tongue. In that moment she was thankful David hadn't left her alone when she wanted him to. She was glad he had been so persistent in getting to know her when he first arrived. She felt a weight lift off her shoulders and off her heart. She had let her burden go, and she had never felt so free.

David drove to his house and parked his dad's car in the driveway. Then he walked Valarie through the orchard to her front porch. Ever since they left the diner he had held on to her hand, as if he was afraid that he would lose her if he let go.

"Did you have a good time?" he asked her, still holding her hand.

Valarie nodded. She did enjoy herself, despite her little meltdown. "Thanks for listening."

He smiled. His eyes sparkled even when they looked tired. "Any time."

Valarie smiled back at him. She wondered how he got the strength to stick with her as long as he had. He must have thought she was worth being around.

She slowly pulled her hand away and started up the front steps. She stopped when she got to the top, wondering if she should carry out her impulse. She turned around and saw David still standing there.

"Good night, Valarie," he said, in a content sort of voice.

"Good night, David."

He smiled then shoved his hands in his pockets and began to walk home. As Valarie turned to go inside she remembered something.

"David!"

He stopped and turned toward her. "Yes?"

"What was the name of the song? The one you were humming along to as we danced?"

He looked downward, and Valarie could tell his tired brain was thinking. "Only You."

She repeated the title in her mind so she wouldn't forget. "Thanks. Good night," she said again then she stood on the porch and watched him as he walked back through the orchard and out of sight. She smiled as she entered her house. The lights were off, except for the lamp near the right side of the couch. Her father was sitting still, and when she walked over to face him, she saw that he had fallen asleep with a book open in his lap. She took the book and set it on the coffee table then she gently touched his hand.

"Dad," she said.

He woke with a groan.

"It's all right. I'm home. You can go to bed now."

"Did you have fun?" he mumbled, clearly still half asleep.

"Yes, Dad. I had fun. I'll tell you all about it in the morning."

"Okay," Tom said with a sigh. He got up and shook himself awake enough to get to his room. He stopped in the doorway and turned toward her, looking a little more awake now that he was on his feet. "Did he kiss you?" he asked.

Valarie smiled at him. "No, Dad," she said, and she was glad she could say it with honesty.

"Good, because he didn't ask for that when he asked me if he could take you to the dance the other day." He yawned.

Valarie was silent. David asked her dad for permission? After all the good he had done for her that night, she had found out he had enough courtesy to ask for her time from someone she said needed her. Suddenly a feeling of joy and admiration swelled inside her. *Oh, David*, she thought, *you're so good to me.*

"Good night, Val," her dad said, and went into his bedroom, leaving her standing in the hallway. She eventually turned and went into the bathroom. She took a quick shower and felt more like herself after she had washed off the makeup and hairspray. She gently placed her necklace on her bedside table as if it was fragile. She stared at it for a moment, and felt David run his hands through her hair. She felt his embrace and his closeness as he tried to kiss her. She suddenly felt stupid. Should she have let him kiss her? Did she panic for no reason? *No*, she told herself, *you did the right thing, and he said he would wait for you, like a gentleman.* She nodded to herself. He was a good gentleman. As she got into bed that night, she pulled out her phone and searched for the song they had danced to. She shoved some ear buds in and listened to the song over and over until she fell asleep. For the first time in a long time, she went to bed with peace.

CHAPTER 9

Valarie awoke the next morning feeling good, in fact, she felt better than she had for a long time, and she went downstairs to breakfast with a smile on her face. Her dad stood at the stove as she entered the kitchen. He turned to her, took one look at her face and laughed.

"Somebody had a good time," he said, with the same smile he had while he gave his tutoring sessions.

"I did have a good time," Valarie agreed.

"So…" her dad drew out the word. "How was the dance?"

"Well, it was fun, even though the music was loud and I had a headache by the end of the night, but it was fun."

"Come on now," Tom said, setting a plate of French toast near the vase with flowers. "Don't spare any details."

Valarie took her usual seat. "There's not much else to tell," she said. "But you can tell me something."

"Oh? What's that?" He set the table with two plates.

"When did David ask for your permission?"

Tom paused as he stood over the sink. Then he laughed. "I was wondering if I had really let that slip last night," he said. He then sat across from her. "About a week ago, David had come to the house before we left to get you to school, in fact he was just about to leave as well, and he only had a few minutes. He asked if it was all right with me if he took you to his senior spring formal, and I told him it was fine. That evening you came home and said that someone had asked you to go with him."

"That's how you knew it was him," Valarie said, putting the pieces together.

"That's also why I said I didn't have anything planned, which I didn't anyway." He let Valarie serve herself then he took his share of the toast. "I want you to do something fun, Val. You're always here, always studying, and you turned down all of your other school dances. I wanted you to experience at least one before you graduate. And David seems like a good kid."

Valarie smiled. She knew he was a good kid.

"And he makes you smile. I haven't seen you smile like that since before…" His voice trailed off. Valarie knew what he was going to say and she knew he was right. After her mom died, all life and happiness seemed to drain from her world. That was until David showed up.

"Well," her dad said. He cleared his throat. "I'm glad you had fun."

Valarie was glad too. She spent the rest of the day with the good feeling in her heart. She wondered what it was about somebody that could make her feel so happy and so carefree. Then it hit her, like a peach falling off the tree and onto her head. *Am I in love?* she asked herself. *Why would I be in love? Hadn't David said he didn't love me? No, what he said was he didn't love me yet. Does that mean he will love me soon?* Her mind wondered over the questions as she browsed among the peach trees in the warm sunshine. It was the best place for her to go where she could think in peace, and something about the plants was soothing to her. She thought of the reasons why she might love David. Was it because he was nice? Kind? Respectful? Handsome? Maybe it was all of the above. Valarie didn't want to admit it, especially to herself, but she thought that maybe her head was right this time. Maybe she was in love. But she was only seventeen, did she even know what love was? She wasn't sure it was what she was feeling; after all, she had never felt it before.

Monday morning came and she couldn't wait for lunchtime to come so she could be with David. After she took her seat, she waited patiently for him to arrive. But he was late. She waited for another fifteen minutes and no sign of him came. Where could he be? Was he all right? Had her worst fear come true and he was now avoiding her? *No,* she told herself, *David said he wouldn't do that, and I believe him.* The day passed without him, and she was disappointed by the time her dad came to take her home.

"You all right, Val? You look a little down," her dad asked, after half the truck ride home had passed in silence.

"Just have a headache," she said, which she did by then from all her worrying. She closed her eyes and leaned her head back on the seat of the truck. *God*, she thought, *please let David be all right. Whoa!* her mind cried. Her eyes popped open. *Did I just pray? Me, a "nonbeliever," so to speak, just asked God for something?* The thought almost made her anxious. Where did that come from? She took a deep breath and tried to reason with herself. *I'm just worried*, she thought. *David is all right, I'm all right, everything's all right.* Suddenly a thought struck her. This wasn't the first time she had prayed before. She remembered the day that she took off school to be with her mother during her illness. Valarie had stood by the bedside, holding her mother's thin and fragile hand, pleading to the Higher Power that she knew her mother believed in to spare her life. But her mother had died that night, and Valarie knew then that no such higher power existed, because if one did, her mother would still be alive. She shook the thought out of her head, and closed her eyes again. It wasn't long before she felt the truck began to slow down.

"Hey, look who it is," her dad said.

She opened her eyes to see a figure walking alongside the road. Her eyes had to adjust to the sunlight, but she knew, without question that the figure was David. He turned around as the truck came to a stop.

"How are you doing?" Tom asked, speaking loud enough for David to hear out Valarie's window.

"I'm all right, sir, how are you?" he asked. A look of exhaustion was smudged across his face.

"I'm pretty good. Why are you walking home?"

"I missed the bus."

Tom nodded. "Well, hop in the truck, we'll take you the rest of the way. Scoot over, Val."

Valarie didn't have to be told twice. She scooted closer to her dad as David got in and set his backpack on his lap.

"Thanks, sir, I appreciate it," he said. He looked even more tired than he had Saturday night.

"No problem," her dad said, driving at regular speed again.

"Are you all right?" Valarie asked in a quiet voice.

"Yeah. I'm sorry I didn't come to sit with you at lunch today, I had to go to the nurses' office."

Valarie's stomach churned. "Are you sick?" she asked, trying not to sound like she was panicking. She had always been afraid of getting sick, but this time, she was more worried about David's health.

"No. I just got a weird headache and felt kind of off. I'll be okay."

Valarie hoped he would recover. She didn't realize how worried about him she was until she saw him try to smile, his eyes blinking slowly.

"My parents would like to invite you two over for dinner sometime this week, if you'd like," he said. Valarie couldn't tell if he was speaking to her or to her dad.

"That sounds great," Tom answered anyway. "Just say when."

"How is Friday evening?"

"I'll check my schedule, but I'm pretty sure we'll be free."

Check your schedule for what? Valarie asked herself. *We don't go anywhere or do anything anyway.*

The ride grew silent, leaving Valarie to her thoughts. A few months ago she was afraid to sit next to David, now it was a comfort to have him near. She could remember the tingling she felt going down her arms and how fast her heart would beat whenever he joined her at lunch. She felt as if she had come a long way from that moment. Of course, she still felt tingling in her arms, but not from nervousness.

"It's all right, you know," Tom said, breaking the silence.

"What's all right?" Valarie asked.

"For you two to hold hands. I don't mind as much as you'd think I would."

He had to say it, she thought. *The car ride was going just fine, now my face is probably red.* She turned to David. He was blushing too.

"Well, Valarie," he said with a smile. "Would you like to hold my hand?"

Valarie tried not to smile, but she couldn't help it. "Yes, I would," she said. David took her hand in his, and Valarie felt the electricity start to flow up her arm into her torso and down her legs. She still wasn't used to the feeling that he gave her. She hoped she would never become used to it.

"There, that wasn't so hard now, was it?" Tom asked. Valarie turned to her dad in time to see a sparkle in his eye. She spent the rest of the truck ride home trying to remember the last time she saw that sparkle.

It was almost ten o'clock that same night and Valarie didn't bother dressing into her pajamas. Her dad had gone to bed early, looking even more tired than usual, and she sat on the foot of her bed with a book open in her lap. What she was really doing was debating on whether or not to go outside to see if David was doing his nightly walk. Maybe he had gone to bed already, after all, he said he wasn't feeling well earlier. Still, she wanted to see him. *Why do you want to see him?* she asked herself. *A month ago you were trying to hide from him. That was different, wasn't it?* Since then he had become her friend, a good friend, and one whom she wanted to spend every spare moment with. *I like him,* she told herself. *Of course you like him,* her mind answered, *think about how happy he makes you, how good he makes you feel,*

all the advice he's given you and all the help he's offered; not to mention the kiss he tried to give you. Valarie put her fingertips to her lips. *What would a kiss feel like?* she wondered. *Why don't you go find out?* her mind said.

Valarie forced herself to walk out of her room, down the stairs, and out of the house, silent as she always was. It felt good to walk outside being calm and collected instead of running to escape her anxiety. She browsed among the peach trees, taking her time to reach the end of the orchard. The peaches trees were beginning to bud, soon they would be covered in blooming flowers, then tiny peaches and the peaches would grow, ripen and be ready to harvest. Valarie knew the cycle all too well.

She didn't see David at the end of the field, so she looked up the hill to his house. There was a single beam of light on the front porch. He must have been sitting on the swing. Valarie went up the hill and slowly approached the porch. David was sitting long ways on the swing with his knees to his chest. He had what looked like a sketch book propped open on bent legs, and his hand was slowly moving across the page. His gaze was focused, and Valarie had never seen him look so intense. When she stopped at the first step, David looked up at her. The single beam of light was a camping lantern, not nearly enough to see his face, but she knew he was smiling at her.

"Hey you," he said. He patted the seat for her to join him. "I was hoping you would find your way over here."

Valarie climbed the steps and noticed that Tiny was seated near the swing. She looked up when Valarie sat and went over to her for attention. "Are you feeling any better?" she asked, scratching Tiny's ears.

David nodded. "Yes, thank you."

Valarie could tell something was wrong with him. He was always an open and honest guy, now he seemed hesitant. Why would he try to hide something from her? Was he sicker than he was letting on? Did something bad happen to him?

"Is there anything I can do for you?" she asked, hoping he would let her in on what was on his mind.

David shook his head. "No, it's okay. I just had a bad day."

Valarie was silent for a moment. She patted the dog on the head one last time then turned toward him. "How can you sketch in the dark?" she asked.

"I always sketch in the dark. My eyes have adapted, I'm like a cat."

"What are you working on?"

David handed her his book and Valarie marveled at what she saw. It was Tiny, lying on the porch with her head on her paws. David had drawn his dog with such detail that Valarie could see every hair on the dog's body, and even the soft glow of her dark eyes.

"This is amazing," she said.

"You think so?" David asked.

"I know so. You got some real talent."

David shrugged his shoulders. "I never really like my art. I always feel like I could do better."

"How can you get any better than this?" she asked. "It's so detailed and...perfect." She looked at David and smiled kindly. His eyes seemed to grow soft and his cheeks began to turn pink.

Valarie handed the book back to him. "What else do you draw?" she asked.

"All kinds of animals," he said. "And sometimes people." He flipped through the pages of his book then handed it to Valarie. She was staring at a portrait of a woman with short light hair, and eyes that sparkled like David's. She was smiling happily with her eyes focused on something in the distance, something that wasn't captured on the page.

"That's my mom," he said. Even on the page, Valarie could see the resemblance between the two. "I drew that about a week ago while she was watching TV. She almost cried when I showed it to her."

Valarie could tell why the woman was brought to tears. "She's beautiful," she said.

David smiled. "You like it?"

She nodded.

David took the book from her and flipped through pages again until he found what he wanted. He handed it back. At first she wondered if she was looking into a mirror, then she gasped when she realized she was staring at her own portrait. David had shaped her soft eyes so that they shined on the page. Her face held a timid smile and her hair was curled like it was the night of the dance. She was in awe.

"I don't think I did you justice." David's voice brought her eyes off the page.

"It's wonderful," she said. "You drew this from memory?"

David nodded. The pink that had appeared on his cheeks had begun to turn bright red. Valarie smiled at his bashfulness.

"Do you have any other hidden talents?"

David shrugged his shoulders again then he said, "I can yodel."

CHAPTER 10

Valarie wasn't sure how she felt about having dinner with David's parents. She was sure they would be nice people, but meeting them made her feel nervous. Would they like her or hate her? Would they ask her all sorts of questions? Would they like her dad? What if conflict arose? What if dinner turns into a disaster? The thoughts were driving around her mind on full speed.

"It will be all right," David said, taking her hand under the lunch table the afternoon of the dinner.

"What if they don't like me?" Valarie couldn't help but asking.

David shook his head. "They'll like you, believe me," he said, caressing her hand. His answer wasn't good enough for her. She wanted to be sure they would like her, not just hope they would. *You're just meeting a friend's parents*, she told herself, *be calm, don't freak out, and everything will be fine.* Once she got home she rummaged the kitchen pantry for something appropriate to take to dinner. Her mother always told her to never to go a dinner empty-handed, unless your host insisted that you don't bring anything. She found various ingredients for chocolate chip cookies and spent the next hour mixing and baking. She put the first batch of cookies in the oven then turned back to cleaning the counter of the flour mess she had made. She paused suddenly, looking at the oven, then at the mixing bowl. She opened the oven and saw that the cookie sheet was there on the top rack then she shut the oven. She looked in the living room and saw her dad sitting on the edge of the couch, going over some papers he brought home from work. In that moment, Valarie realized that she had forgotten all about her fear of using the oven. She had always had her dad put the pans in the oven for her, for she was afraid of getting burned. But now that she was determined to make a good impression for someone, she had overcome one and she didn't even know it. She could have jumped for joy over her little victory. Instead she just smiled, finished baking, and arranged the cookies on the prettiest plate she could find. Then she went upstairs to her room, brushed her hair, and sprayed a dose of her mother's perfume on her shirt. She checked to make sure the cross necklace was in place in the center of her neck then she went downstairs and announced to her dad that she was ready. The two left the house and walked on the outskirt of the orchard. Her father didn't like walking through the trees unless he was checking on the produce.

"Are you nervous?" he asked, breaking the silence.

Valarie shook her head. "No," she said. *It's not a lie*, she told herself, *I'm not nervous, I'm terrified, there's a difference.*

"You know, when I first met your mother's parents, I thought I was going to throw up."

Valarie sighed. "Is that supposed to be inspiring?" she asked. She looked at her dad to see a smile on his face.

"No," he answered. "I just knew that she meant a lot to me if I was that nervous about impressing her parents."

Valarie felt the sting of tears in her eyes. She knew her dad loved her mom with all his heart, and it must have taken everything in him to not break down whenever he spoke of her.

"How did that evening go?" she asked, wanting to hear more.

Her dad looked off in the distance. "Pretty well actually," he said. "You know how well Grandma can cook. Good food always seems to help the nerves."

Valarie nodded in agreement. Grandma certainly made the best homemade chicken and dumplings soup in the world.

"Were you afraid Grandma and Grandpa wouldn't like you?"

Her dad stopped in his tracks, causing Valarie to stop too. "I was terrified," he said. His voice was soft, yet serious.

"But, I tried to be as polite as I could. I told myself that they raised the woman I loved to be all that she could be, and in return they deserved my respect."

Valarie wondered where such advice was coming from. Her dad was never one to be sentimental, yet he seemed to speak from experience.

"What if they don't like me?" she asked.

Her dad smiled. "Then they are blind and can't see a good thing when it's right in front of them." He patted Valarie on the back. "Come on," he said, continuing to walk. "First impressions are very important. You don't want to be late."

Valarie's heart began to speed up with each step she took toward the house. She had been to the front porch many times, but this time it felt new and different. She was going to walk into the place where David lived and get a glimpse of his world. Lights shining from the inside seemed to glow through the white lace curtains on the glass doors with brown wood outlines. She could hear music playing from somewhere, it almost sounded like country. She rang the doorbell and stepped back a few feet. Taking a deep breath she braced herself.

The outline of someone tall came to the door. A woman answered, wearing a bright pink apron and a wide smile. Valarie recognized her from the portrait David had sketched. He had captured her face flawlessly.

"Valarie," she said. Her voice was soft and welcoming. Suddenly Valarie saw her mother's face and wished she was with her. She put on her brightest smile. "Yes, ma'am. And this is my father, Tom."

"I'm Nancy, Nancy Summers," the woman said, shaking her hand, then her father's. "Well, come on in. Make yourselves comfortable."

Valarie slowly entered the house and paused. Even though it looked a bit rustic on the outside, it was a palace inside. Three large brown cloth couches with wooden feet sat on a pale blue rug on the floor. Two large end tables were glistening from wood gloss in the light of the chandelier hanging overhead. An antique lamp sat on one of the tables, and an entertainment center, taller than Valarie to the right of the front door with a TV as wide as both her arms outstretched. A tall cabinet with glass trinkets leaned against the wall on the stairs and a bookshelf sat next to it. The home defiantly had a woman's touch, a mother's touch. For a split second Valarie almost felt jealous.

She turned to Mrs. Summers and held out the plate of cookies. "I made a dessert for after dinner."

Mrs. Summers smiled wide. "Thank you, that's very kind. Just make yourselves at home, we'll be right out." She took the plate and disappeared into the kitchen through a swinging door. Valarie wandered into the dining room, where a long, dark mahogany table sat in the center. Five ivory cloth placemats were set with plates, silverware and tall glass cups. Candles and flowers decorated the center, and Valarie picked up the scent of roast beef and garlic bread. Her stomach growled. She was hungry after all.

She heard a door close behind her, and turned to see David. Seeing him was comforting, and she breathed a sigh of relief.

"Hey," he said to her, giving her a hug. "I'm glad you two could make it."

"Thanks for inviting us," Valarie said. "You've got a beautiful home."

David looked around as if he hadn't noticed it before. "Thanks." He leaned closer to Valarie and whispered, "I personally think the place is a little girly, but my mom rules the roost."

Valarie smiled.

David turned to her dad. "How are you, sir?" he said. The tone of his voice changed from comfortable to courteous.

"I'm doing pretty well. How are you?"

David shrugged. "Hungry."

"Me too." Tom agreed. "Do you do any cooking?"

"A little. My mom insists on teaching me, so she has me cook something new at least once a day."

"That's good. When you get out on your own you won't have to live off of pizza and burgers."

"True that," David said.

The door swung open again and out came Mrs. Summers, carrying a platter of roast beef. "David, honey, will you bring out the bowl of potatoes please," she asked, arranging the plate on the table.

David smiled at Valarie then went into the kitchen. He came out a moment later with a bowl of steaming boiled potatoes. A man, taller than Nancy, followed him out with a bowl of sliced garlic bread.

"Hi," he said in a booming voice. He set the bowl down then went to shake her father's hand. "I'm Rodger," the man said.

"Tom," her father said with a nod.

He turned to Valarie and smiled. "Now, this young lady must be the famous Valarie. David has told us much about you."

Valarie felt the heat of the bowl on his skin as he shook his hand. "All good things, I hope," She said, shooting David a look of uncertainty. He winked at her, as if he was telling her not to be worried.

Mr. Summers paused and a sincere look came across his face. "All great things," he said. He let go of her hand.

"Well, if everybody is ready to eat, I say we sit and eat," Mrs. Summers said. Mr. Summers pulled out a chair for his wife. A red color appeared on her delicate skin and Valarie could tell that the gesture made her feel special. Mr. Summers sat next to her at the head of the table. Tom sat himself next to Mr. Summers as David pulled a chair out for Valarie next to her dad. He sat next to her at the other end of the table.

David took her hand then reached across the table for his mother's hand. Mrs. Summers took her husband's hand, and Valarie recognized what was about to take place. She remembered her mother insisting on saying grace before eating the meals she cooked. Her father never seemed to be for it, but he didn't tell anyone. He would hold her hand and listen as she prayed, and he would pray over the meal whenever she asked him to. Valarie took her father's hand and wondered when the last time her family had prayed. Mr. Summers bowed his head and gave thanks over the meal. He thanked God for the gathering of friends and for bringing Valarie into his son's life. Valarie felt David squeeze her hand as if he was telling her that he agreed with his father. It had been a long time since Valarie heard someone say that they were thankful for her presence. She felt so invisible and shy everywhere she went that she assumed no one would ever be happy that she was around. She hadn't felt that since her mom died. She tried not to break down and cry at the Summers' dinner table.

CHAPTER 11

Valarie had forgotten all about being nervous as the dinner carried slowly into the evening. Mr. and Mrs. Summers had asked her what her hobbies were, her favorite books, and what she planned on doing when she graduated high school next year. David's parents seemed interested in her life, and they were encouraging when she replied that she was unsure about college. They smiled a lot, and shared many funny stories about silly things David had done when he was a child. They made her feel welcome, like she was already a part of their family.

Mrs. Summers rose to clear the table and Valarie offered to help. She gathered the dinner plates and followed Mrs. Summers into the kitchen.

"Just place them in the sink," the woman said. She walked to the refrigerator and pulled out a cake plate.

"Would you hand me five small plates from the cupboard up there," she said, pointing above the stove.

Valarie did as asked and watched as Mrs. Summers began to slice a chocolate cake. Valarie felt full from the delicious dinner, but she wasn't going to pass up a piece of cake.

"That looks delicious," Valarie couldn't help but saying.

Mrs. Summers smiled. "Thank you, but I didn't make it. David did."

"Really? David made this?" Valarie didn't believe it. He had more hidden talents than he admitted to.

Mrs. Summers nodded, dishing a third slice. "I've been teaching him how to cook, so that when he goes to college he'll know how to feed himself. I think if it were up to him he'd choose to live off of take out for the rest of his life." She took the plate of cookies that Valarie brought and put one on each plate. "At first he was dreading it, and he burned everything he tried to bake."

Valarie laughed.

"But, over time, he got the hang of things around the kitchen. Now, he's a real chef." She re-covered the cookies and set them aside.

"He once told me about the time he forgot to grease the muffin pan before he poured the batter in and set it in the oven to bake," Valarie said, trying to keep the conversation going.

Mrs. Summers laughed. "I remember that. We had to scrape the muffins out with a spoon. But they just crumbled so we sprinkled them over some ice cream. All in all, they were pretty good muffins." She set the plates on the counter and sighed. Valarie waited for her to speak, but the woman was silent. She turned to look at Valarie and a faint smile appeared across her face. "That's a beautiful necklace," she said.

Valarie touched the pendant. "David gave it to me."

Mrs. Summers smiled. "I know. I was with him when he picked it out for you. Just between you and me, he spent almost an hour trying to find something to get you. He said he wanted something beautiful for a beautiful girl," she smiled. "He was right, Valarie. You sure are lovely."

Valarie felt her face grow hot. "Thank you," she said, not knowing what else to say. Mrs. Summers turned back to the counter and paused. Valarie waited for her to hand her a plate or two, but the woman hesitated. Her eyes fell to the floor and Valarie saw an unexplainable expression on her face. "Valarie," she said, almost sounding as if she was going to cry. "I want you to know something. I was debating on whether or not to tell you, because it is rather personal for David, but after some time in prayer, and seeing how he seems to really like you, I thought you should know."

Valarie felt her arms go numb. The woman sounded sad, and she wondered if all the talk and laughter over dinner was going to fade away. She braced herself for the worst things that Mrs. Summers could possibly tell her.

"David is a good kid, but he's been through a lot," she began, not taking her eyes off the plates of dessert. "Over a year ago, David was dating this girl at the high school he attended when we lived in Colorado," she paused for a breath. "About six months into the relationship, the girl killed herself, and for while after that, David was very distressed."

Valarie felt her chest get tight, as if an elephant was sitting on her. A lump began to rise in her throat and she felt as if she was suffocating.

"He's doing much better now. But for a while he was having anxiety and guilt over her death. The girl was a good girl. I personally never would have guessed that she was hurting so much on the inside as to take her own life. But she did. She didn't tell anyone. One day I got a call from the girl's mother saying that the girl was found dead in her room, under the covers of her own bed. The girl's mother tried to wake her for school that morning, but the girl was already gone. She had swallowed a bottle of pills the night before and fell into a deep sleep, never to wake up."

Valarie's stomach churned. She could feel tears began to sting her eyes, and she wanted more than anything to turn and run home.

"I just want you to know that he likes you, a lot," Mrs. Summers continued, finally facing her. There were tears in her eyes. "And losing a girlfriend really hurt him. As his mother, all I ask of you is if you don't like him, let him know, please don't lead him on and then dump him in the gutter. I can't watch my boy suffer again. Can you do that, for me, and for him?"

Valarie felt a hot tear roll down her cheek. She didn't know that David had been through something as traumatic as losing a friend to suicide. *Why didn't he tell me?* she asked herself. *Does he not want me to know?* She nodded to Mrs. Summers, letting her know that she understood. Mrs. Summers reached out and wiped the tear from Valarie's face.

"He does really like you," the woman said. "And you seem to make him very happy. I just don't want him to get hurt again."

Valarie tried to swallow the lump in her throat. "He makes me happy too," she said, getting control over her voice.

Mrs. Summers turned back to the dessert plates. "All right," she said. "Let's get these out to the boys, and try to enjoy the rest of our evening."

Valarie followed Mrs. Summers back out to the dining room. She still hadn't fully processed what she had just been told, and the bizarre feeling of it all made her want to run up to David and wrap her arms around him and tell him she was sorry for his loss. She served him a plate then sat next to him. She turned and looked at him for a moment, and felt as if she wasn't in the dining room in his house, but somewhere far off, away from parents of sorrow and pain. She gazed deep into his eyes for what felt like forever then she turned her attention to the cake she no longer felt like eating.

"Thanks again for having us over for dinner," Valarie said, as she and her father walked down the front steps.

"Any time. Thank you for coming," Mr. Summers said. They stood near the railing of their front porch to say good-bye. David had asked if he could walk them home, and despite Valarie's desire to be away from him for a little while, his parents agreed.

Tom had walked on ahead of them, saying he felt tired. Valarie walked with David in silence, not sure if she should tell him she knew about his girlfriend, or if she should just keep the information to herself. Either way it started to eat at her, and she could feel the anxiety she worked so hard to recover from start to creep back into her mind.

"Are you all right? You've been quiet since dessert." David gently took her hand. His skin was hot compared to hers.

"I just have a headache," she said. Then she felt even worse for lying to him.

"Are you sure that's all?"

Valarie could tell he didn't believe her, but she didn't want to tell him what she knew. Not yet. She nodded to him, keeping her eyes on the path that led around the orchard.

The two were silent for a moment then David asked. "Did my mom say something that upset you?"

Valarie shook her head. "I'm all right, really." She looked at him and tried to smile.

The look on his face told her that he still didn't believe her, but she tried to smile as if what she knew wasn't eating her up inside. The two walked in silence to her house. Tom was waiting at the front door when they stopped near the porch.

"Thanks again," Valarie said. She let go of his hand and walked up the steps. She could feel David watching her, but she didn't look back. She walked straight inside, put the cookie plate in the sink and announced that her head hurt and she wanted to go lie down. She said good night to her dad then went up to her attic room. After shutting the door, she leaned against it for a while, replaying in her head all that Mrs. Summers had told her. She could still see the woman's sad expression and tear-filled eyes. She barely knew Valarie and she had shared something so personal and heartbreaking with her. Why had she shared the story with her? Did his mother think that David liked her that much as to let her know about what had happened to him? Was she trying to scare Valarie away? Tears began to stream down her face again, and she wondered how she was going to face David without telling him what she knew. Would he be upset if she told him she knew? Would that ruin what they had just started to share? Her heart broke for him. She had dealt with death before, but not with intentional death. That was how he knew so much about coping with death and grief; that was how he was able to help Valarie with her anxiety like he was reading her mind. She had been honest with him about not knowing how a relationship worked, about how she wasn't sure if she liked him. He seemed to be okay with that. He never pushed her for anything; accept to keep trying to not let fear get in her way of living her life. Life seemed so precious to him. She seemed precious to him, as if he didn't want to lose another girlfriend. Valarie couldn't stay with him if she didn't love him, she couldn't be mean to him like that. What would David do if she told him that a relationship wasn't going to work? She didn't think he would harm himself, would he? The thoughts racing through her head made it start to ache for real. She walked over to her shelf and began to pick out something to sleep in. How was she going to face him Monday? Just act like nothing had happened? She had tried doing that with her mother's death, and it ate her up every single day. With all the force she had in her thin arm, she threw a shirt on the bed and began to cry. She hated death. Death seemed to ruin everything in a person's life. Her mother died, but at least she had her dad. David's first girlfriend died, and who did he have? His parents? Her? Suddenly a thought struck Valarie's mind, one that almost took her breath away. Did he only like her because he wanted somebody? Did she remind him of his first girlfriend? Was she a replacement? *No*, she told herself, *no, no, no*. She wasn't even going to entertain the thought. She would act like she was fine until she felt it was time to let him know, or until he opened up about it himself, whichever situation came first.

CHAPTER 12

Valarie woke on Monday morning with a heavy heart. She had spent Sunday inside, trying to avoid David until she processed what had happened to him. Now, she knew she had to face him. She could remember the last time she tried to avoid him, going to extremes such as trying to fake a stomach ache. But she had faced him back then and she was going to face him now. Maybe all that she was told would just blow away once she saw him. *What if it didn't?* she wondered, but she would never know unless she tried. Normally she wasn't so eager to try, but she didn't want to lose David. She needed closer. She needed to know what she could do to make a relationship work, and for the first time in her life, she was determined to try harder than just wishful thinking.

The day passed smoothly until lunchtime came. The two sat together and Valarie tried not to see his mother's tearful face every time she looked at him. She complimented him on his cooking skills, and asked what other foods he had mastered in the kitchen.

"I've pretty much nailed foods like pasta, sandwiches, and breakfasts, those are easy. I like cooking foods that I can add flavor and spice and my own soul into, you know? I can whip up a killer meatloaf, with peppers and tomatoes. I should make it for you sometime," he said.

"Maybe you should go to into culinary arts," Valarie suggested.

"I thought about it," David said, pushing his lunch tray aside, already having finished his lunch. "But my heart is with helping people. If I can help somebody, even with something small, I'll be a happy camper." He wiped his mouth. "It's not about money or popularity, it's about life and its beauty. Too many people suffer and lots of time, no one knows about it until it's too late. Other times, people know and they don't care. The world doesn't need any more critics. We need to be kind and help people to the best of our abilities. That's why I was eager to help you, because I saw that you needed someone to talk to, and I know what it's like to feel alone and broken."

Valarie wondered if he only helped her because he felt guilty for his girlfriend's death.

The sun had barely set when Valarie's father declared he was going to bed. He seemed to be making his bedtime earlier and earlier with each passing day. Even though his job didn't work him hard physically, Valarie could tell that he was always tired. He seemed to have never recovered from the stress and exhaustion of losing his wife. *Loss, such a painful, useless thing*, Valarie thought. *All it does is rob us of good people and makes us forget what it was like to be happy.* She sat on the couch for a while, flipping through TV channels in an attempt to occupy her mind. When that didn't work, she turned the TV off and picked up the book on the coffee table, the one her dad had been reading. It was one of those Dickens classics that he seemed to enjoy over all other genres. For lack of something better to do, she took the book outside and sat on the first step of the front porch and tried to read in what little light the porch lamp let off. She was just at the part where Pip was getting scolded by his aunt for coming home late, when she heard footsteps nearby. She looked up and saw David approaching her.

"Hey, frog," he said.

"Frog?" Valarie drowned out the word. "Where did that come from?"

"I was watching a documentary about frogs on one of those educational channels. It was the first thing that came to mind just now."

Valarie laughed. David was a good kid, but he sure was a nut. "So I remind you of a big, ugly frog?"

"No, you're more like one of the green tree frogs with fierce eyes and beautiful colors."

Valarie scooted over and patted the step. "I've never been fierce in my life."

"That day will come. One moment you'll be wondering what on earth is happening, then you'll do something so brave you'll amaze everybody, including yourself."

Valarie was quiet. She almost hoped she would never experience being fierce.

"What are you reading?" David asked.

Valarie closed the book and handed it to him. "It's one of my dad's. He loves those classics. He said he grew up reading them over and over."

"I've read every Dickens novel there is," David said, handing the book back.

"I try to read classics, but I just end up falling asleep," she confessed. "They don't hook me like modern fiction does."

"You just got to find one that interests you." He smiled at her, and the sparkles in his eyes appeared like stars in the dark. "Why are you trying to read with no light?"

Valarie shrugged. "I needed something to do."

"Well, I have come to rescue you from your boredom," he said, as if he was a proper English gentleman. "I was wondering if you'd like to play cards." He held out a deck of old-fashioned playing cards.

"Sure," Valarie said. She put her book aside. David shuffled the deck and began to teach her how to play poker using assorted pebbles he had collected as betting money. After half an hour the sky was completely dark and David had won every game they played.

"What happened to beginner's luck?" Valarie asked, feeling a little resentful.

"I don't know," David said, separating his pile of newly won pebbles according to their size. "At least we aren't playing with real money this time."

"Yeah, I'd be broke by now," Valarie said. She looked up and fixed her gaze on the dark night sky. It was a clear night with only a handful of scattered stars. She stared for a while until she heard David's voice.

"What?" she asked, meeting his eyes.

"What are you thinking about?" he repeated.

Valarie shook her head. "Nothing, I'm just admiring the sky."

David looked up. "It's too bad there aren't more stars out tonight. It would be perfect for stargazing."

Valarie looked at David to see him staring at her. His eyes were sharp in the pale porch light, yet his face was content. He seemed to be happy every time she saw him. She wondered how he got through losing his girlfriend. Did he still feel guilty and blame himself? Did he still miss her? Had he loved her? She tried to block the questions out, not wanting to think about them, but at the same time she would have given anything to have all the answers.

"Valarie," David said. "You remember when you said you didn't know how a relationship works, and I told you I could help you along the way?"

Valarie nodded.

"Well, part of being in a relationship is being open and honest with each other. I can tell something is bothering you, and that it had been bothering you ever since my parents had you over for dinner. Whatever it is, you can tell me, and maybe we can work it out together."

Valarie felt tears sting her eyes. She felt like she had swallowed a bomb and was just waiting to explode. She still didn't know how to explain her feelings, other than to let them out all at once, but she needed to do it delicately this time, or else she would blow.

David gathered the cards and set them aside. He moved closer to Valarie and took her hand. "It's okay," he said softly. "Don't keep it inside. I can tell it's hurting you."

A tear rolled down Valarie's cheek, and a lump was rising in her throat. She was blocked now, cornered. She had to let him know; otherwise she might lose what they just started to share.

She opened her mouth to speak, but the words wouldn't come. She couldn't even think of the right thing to say. *How should I start? Hey, I'm sorry about your girlfriend that killed herself. Am I her replacement? Yeah, that's delicate*, her mind told her.

"Was it something I said that night?" David asked.

Valarie shook her head.

"Something my mom said?"

Valarie paused. She didn't want him to be angry with his mother; after all, she was only looking out for him.

"Is that a yes?"

Valarie nodded.

"What did she say? Did she tell you that you're not good for me?"

Valarie shook her head again.

"Did she say she didn't like you?"

"No."

He paused, as if he was thinking about what else it could be that was bothering her. "I'm at a loss, Valarie, you can just tell me."

"I'm not sure if you want me to know."

"Know what?"

"What she told me."

"What did she tell you?"

Valarie hesitated. "I don't want you to be angry with her for telling me."

A kind smile came across David's face and he let out a sigh mixed with a laugh. "Valarie, I promise I won't get mad at anyone. I just want to know what's bothering you so I can help you with it." Then he added in an almost sarcastic tone of voice. "Communication is the number one thing to a good relationship, you know."

Valarie wiped the tears from her face. She knew he was only trying to lighten the mood, but he wasn't helping. Now she wished he hadn't told her that. Now she would have to let loose the knowledge of what happened to him. She felt David's hand give hers a gentle squeeze. With his other hand he moved her brown hair behind her ears. She loved the feeling of his fingers in her hair. It was comforting and it gave her the feeling of acceptance. He leaned his forehead against hers. "You don't have to be afraid," he whispered. "You don't have to hide the hurt from me. Please, Mandy."

Mandy? Valarie wondered if she heard him correctly. Had he just called her by someone else's name? Or was she just imagining what he was saying to her? *No, I know what I heard,* she told herself. She was sure of it. She looked up and caught his gaze. "Who's Mandy?" she asked cautiously. Her voice so soft it sounded like a whisper.

David's smile disappeared and his eyebrows pulled together in confusion. He stared at her for a moment before asking, "Where did you hear that name?"

"You called me Mandy, just now," she explained.

David's face froze. "I did?" he asked, barely moving his lips.

Valarie nodded.

David looked down at her hand and slowly placed it on her lap, as if it was a dead animal that he didn't want to touch. He faced the dirt driveway and stared out at something Valarie couldn't see. His breathing became shallow, and by the look on his face, Valarie wondered if he was in pain, or trying not to hit something. Suddenly David stood to his feet and rushed down the steps. He walked a little down the driveway, walked back up to the porch, then turned and walked back down the driveway again. He paced like this for a few minutes as if he was deep in thought, like trying to solve a riddle. Valarie saw that he was containing some kind of emotion. She hoped he wouldn't blow up with anger.

He stopped at the bottom step and lifted his face to her. Tears were spilling out of his eyes and streaming down his face. Valarie had never seen him look distressed or sad before, and there he was, crying at her doorstep. Suddenly she felt helpless. She wasn't sure if she was supposed to comfort him or just let him be, let him release whatever was about to blow. She swallowed hard, then slowly rose to her feet, met him at the bottom step, and gently put her arms around him to hold him. She was afraid that he would push her away, but instead she felt his body relax in her arms as he started to sob. After he released his emotions, he took her hand and led her into the orchard.

CHAPTER 13

"Mandy was my first girlfriend," David said, keeping his eyes on the dirt path he was walking on. "We got together in my junior year in at a high school I attended in Colorado. I was like you back then, not really sure how a relationship should work, but neither did she. We figured being boyfriend and girlfriend was just like being best friends, so we decided to give it a try."

Valarie kept quiet and gave David the space he needed talk.

"One day, about four months into the 'relationship,' she appeared sad and downcast to me. I knew something was wrong, because she had always been a happy-go-lucky type of person. I assumed she was just not feeling good, so I let her be. About two weeks later, she was still the same. I asked her what was wrong, but she told me that it was nothing, so I just let it go. But I started to realize that she wasn't the same. She didn't smile anymore, she didn't laugh, and she didn't even want to go out with me anymore, so I thought maybe I was doing something wrong. I bought her flowers, gave her little gifts, and told her she looked pretty and all, thinking that she just needed some attention to get back to her normal self. It helped her for a little while, but she was back to being sad the following week. Finally I called her up and told her that she needed to tell me what was wrong, that maybe I could help her, because I didn't know how to deal with her mood changes. She asked me to meet her at the park and she would explain everything then. So I did. We sat on a bench and I waited for what felt like hours for her to tell me what was wrong. Then she..." David's voice cracked. He was trying to contain his sobs long enough to speak.

"She lifted her shirt, up to her torso, and I see this big, baseball-sized bruise the left side of her ribcage. I was shocked. I asked her what happened, and she started to cry. She tells me that her dad hit her. She didn't tell me why, only that she didn't do something he wanted her to do. I told her we should call the police, get some help, but she insisted on just letting the matter go. But I couldn't let it go. I couldn't stand by and watch as my girlfriend was abused and act as if nothing was happening."

David stopped in his tracks. He fixed his eyes on a peach tree and continued, "So a few days later, I go to my parents. I tell them what I saw and heard, and they go to

Mandy's parents. Her father denied it, of course, but the bruise was still there, on her ribs. She told my parents that she fell in the bathroom. I couldn't believe it. There I was, trying to help her out of a life and death situation, and she refused any help, making me out to be a liar. I was stunned."

He paused to wipe his nose, still staring at the tree. "The next day she doesn't show up to school. The day after that, I see her in the cafeteria. I go up to her, ask her why she didn't accept any help, but she tells me that our relationship is over, and that she never wants to see me again. But I couldn't let it go, not when she was being treated that way. I know now that she was only scared of being hurt even more, and that she was walking on eggshells everyday just to avoid another beating. So I go to my parents, and we go to the police station, but they told us that unless Mandy confesses to being beaten, they couldn't do anything about the situation. So I try to get Mandy to come out, say that she's abused and that she wants help, but she's avoiding me at all costs. Finally, I threw the towel in. I told her that I couldn't help someone who didn't want to be helped, I told her that I give up." His voice cracked again. He turned to Valarie and fixed his eyes on hers.

"I get called out of school the next morning, and my mom tells me that Mandy was found dead, in her bed, with a bottle of pills on the floor." He began to sob heavily. "She was in her pajamas, under her covers as if she was tucked in for a good night's sleep. When they moved her, they found fresh bruising on her arms and stomach. Her dad had just finished beating her the night before."

Valarie felt tears spill out of her own eyes as she listened. David turned away from her and continued to cry. "She was helpless," he said, in a loud and pain filled voice. "I tried to help her but I gave up. I gave up! I didn't see how much she was hurting and how afraid she was. I shouldn't have given up!" He swung his arm and hit the peach tree with his fist. Valarie heard a cracking sound and wondered if it was the bark or his fingers that broke. He kicked at the trunk, over and over until he exhausted himself. Then he leaned against the trunk and cried some more. "I shouldn't have given up," he said in a low voice, almost as if he was talking to himself. "If I hadn't given up, she would still be alive today."

Valarie watched as he let gravity take hold of him and slid down the trunk of the tree, landing on his backside. He sat quiet for a while, with his head leaned to his right, resting against the trunk. Tears continuing to stream down his face. Valarie stood frozen, wondering if he had let out all his built up emotions. She felt sorry for him all over again. The poor boy felt guilty for a death he didn't even know was going to happen, yet he screamed and shouted as if he was confessing he had shoved the pills down the poor girl's throat. He felt responsible, and he blamed himself for her death. Valarie had no idea how to comfort him. She walked over to him, and slowly sat next to him. She wiped his face. David opened his eyes and turned to her. He swallowed. "I wanted to help you, because I saw that you were hurting, that you were a prisoner to some kind of emotional pain, and I would rather die than to see someone hurting and not help them. I can't let another Mandy walk by and let her go on her way knowing that I could have done something. Maybe if I could help you, then God would somehow forgive me for giving up on her."

Valarie saw a look of pain in his eyes that she had never seen before. It took the blue color away and replaced it with a dark and cloudy grey. Her heart broke at the sea of guilt that his eyes reflected.

"It's not your fault," she said, not knowing what else to tell him. "You tried to help, but you're right, you can't help someone who isn't willing to help themselves." She knew that from all the self-help books she had read.

"I gave up on her, Valarie," David said, sounding unconvinced. "I shouldn't have let her go."

"You tried everything, going to her parents and the police. What else could you have done?"

"I should have stood by her side, even if that meant waiting for her to want help."

"She may never have wanted help, David. She may have taken her own life whether you gave up or not. But you tried, and you can't blame yourself for someone else's actions."

David closed his eyes.

"It's not your fault," Valarie whispered.

"Then whose fault is it?" The tone of his voice let her know that he was becoming irritated with being told that he wasn't to blame.

She was quiet for a moment then she said, "It's the fault of whatever drove her to suicide. Not of the only person who tried to help her." She gently placed a hand on his cheek and pulled his face toward her. He slowly blinked his eyes, still cloudy with tears. "I don't know much about God, but I don't think He blames you for what happened to her. And I don't think he'd want you to blame yourself either." The dark grey in his eyes began to clear, as if the sun had come out. She let go of him, feeling that her message had gotten through to him.

David sighed heavily. "That's what the counselor said." His eyes were puffy and no matter how many times he wiped the tears off of his face they just kept flowing. He looked at Valarie and tried to smile, but it wasn't his usual happy smile. He reached out and touched Valarie's cheek, like she had done a moment before. "Why did God let me cross your path?" he asked.

Valarie wondered if he was talking to himself. She thought of something to say, but all she could think of was, "I don't know. Maybe you needed to hear that it wasn't your fault from a friend, not a parent or professional."

David pulled his hand back. "I'm sorry," he said, starting to sob again.

Valarie shook her head. "Don't be sorry," she said. "You've been strong for a while now, and you just needed a break."

David wiped his face again. He seemed to recognize the words she spoke as the exact words he told her when she broke down about her mother. "I meant I'm sorry for calling you by her name. I know that's not who you are."

Valarie swallowed the lump in her throat. "It's okay. But you're not superman, you can't save everybody." She choked back a sob. "My mom said that's what God is for."

David nodded. "Your mother is right." He breathed in deep, as if cleansing out his lungs from the words he just spoke. "I know I can't save anyone, but I wish I could have saved her."

Valarie was silent. She still wasn't sure what she should do, so she did the only thing she could think of. She held his hand and said, "Please don't blame yourself. You didn't kill her, and you don't need to save anybody to redeem yourself."

"Do you believe in God, Valarie?"

Valarie didn't know what to say. She didn't know if she did believe. "My mother did."

"Do you?"

Valarie shrugged her shoulders. "I don't know."

"I think you do. You talk like you do."

"I asked God to spare my mother, and she died anyway. I don't think a higher power would have let her die."

"I used to wonder why God let Mandy do that to herself. But people were telling me that everything happens for a reason then they said that I may know need to know the reason why things happen."

Valarie shook her head. "I bet that helped," she said sarcastically.

Her comment brought a smile to David's face. "It's been hard."

"I know," Valarie said. "And it really hurts."

"I know," David said. The two sat in silence for a while then Valarie wrapped her arms around his neck and held him close. "It will be all right," she said. "You don't have to feel guilty anymore, just like I don't have to feel afraid."

CHAPTER 14

Valarie woke the next morning to her usual ringing alarm, yet it somehow sounded much louder to her ears. Her body felt exhausted, as if she hadn't slept at all, and her eyes burned when she blinked them open. She would have given anything to spend the day in bed and not have to get up and face whatever challenge the day was going to throw at her. Yet she knew that if she didn't get up, her dad would come to check on her and would insist on taking her to a doctor. She didn't know what motivated her to get up, but she threw the blankets off to the side and sat on the edge of her bed for a few minutes. She soon realized that the wood flooring was cold on the soles of her feet. She unwillingly stood and went to her dresser and pulled out a pair of socks then she sat back down on her bed to put them on. She sighed heavily, wondering how David was feeling that morning. Maybe he would stay home from school on the excuse that his head was hurting again. Sometimes she felt jealous of his ability to hide his feelings.

Dragging herself out of bed, Valarie dressed and went into the bathroom to brush her hair. She pulled out her makeup bag from under the sink and brushed on a little eye shadow, hoping it would cover the puffiness. She sprayed on a dose of perfume, feeling like she needed some comfort from the only person that was no longer there for her. She hardly touched the breakfast that her dad had made and she hardly spoke a word on the way to school. Her father pulled into the shoulder and put the truck in park. She started to get out when her dad asked, "Is something wrong, Val?"

She wanted to blurt out, "Yes, Dad, something is very wrong, my boyfriend thinks the suicide of his first girlfriend is his own fault and I spent half the night trying to convince him that it wasn't." She wondered what he would say to that. "No," she said plainly. "I'm just real tired."

"Are you sure?"

Valarie nodded.

"All right," he said. "See you at four."

For the first time in a while, he looked as if he didn't believe her. But Valarie didn't sit around long enough to ask if he did or not. She got out of the truck and went straight inside without stopping to stare down the building that entrapped her every day. She wanted to go in, get through her lessons, and get out. She made her way through the hall and to English class when she saw David outside the door, talking to Eric. He turned when she approached the door, and Valarie saw that his eyes were tired and swollen as well. His usual smile was gone and his appearance seemed to lack the happy energy he usually let off. He quietly watched Valarie as she grew closer, ignoring whatever Eric was trying to tell him. Valarie hoped she could walk past him and into the classroom without stopping to talk to him, but she knew it was too late for that. She felt a hand gently grab her arm as she reached for the door.

"Hey," David said, even his voice sounded tired. "Can I talk to you real quick?"

Valarie looked down at her feet. She didn't want to meet his eyes. "Maybe later, I need to get inside." She felt him release her and she hurried inside the classroom without saying another word. She stormed to the back of the class and dropped into her seat. She glanced up at the clock. It was ten minutes till eight. She could have stayed and talked to David but she didn't want him to say anything about last night. She wanted to get it as far away from her mind as possible. She folded her arms on the desk and laid her head on the cold wood. She could tell that it was going to be a long day. Her head shot up at the sound of something crashing outside the classroom. A few students looked around at each other, as if wondering if anyone else heard the noise. A yell came from outside the door, and one boy jumped up and went to the door to look out of the narrow glass window.

"There's a fight going on out there," he said, without taking his eyes away from the window.

Valarie shot out of her seat and to the door, pushing the kid aside as she looked out. To her horror, Eric had shoved David into a locker, pinning him against the metal. He was trying to get free. A crowd of students had gathered, already shouting for a fight. Valarie swung the door open and pushed through the circle just in time for David to punch Eric right in the face, making him release his hold. Eric bent over with his hands to his face. His eyes were shut tight from the pain. Afraid that he would swing back at David, Valarie leaped forward in an attempt to stop him. She felt a hand grab hers, as if someone was trying to hold her back, but she didn't stop to find out. She stepped between the two and faced Eric just in time for a fist to come down on her left cheekbone. The blow drove her to the floor and she saw the world go dark for a few seconds before she could make out the shape of things. She saw David pinning Eric to the wall just as Eric had done to him moments before. He gave him one punch, then another, and another. Eric didn't have a second to fight back.

"Stop," she said, in a weak voice. No one heard her over the sound of the screaming students. She put a hand to her head. It was already throbbing. She got to her hands and knees, trying to stand to her feet, but her head was dizzy. She fell on onto her backside, and leaned against some lockers. Someone knelt next to her and took her arm. Valarie had to concentrate hard to see that it was Emma. She looked frightened.

"Are you okay?" she asked.

Valarie shook her head. She couldn't answer her, she had to see where David was. She looked out at where he had been standing last and saw that a few teachers had stepped in and separated the two. David was wiping blood from his nose while Eric was glaring at him through eyes that were starting to swell. Blood was running down his lip, and he looked ready for another fight. David had beaten him hard. He looked at Valarie, and she noticed that the skin on the right side of his cheekbone was busted open. His eyes reflected sympathy, and he started for her, but the teacher held his arm out and to keep him back. The teacher turned to her and pointed to Emma.

"Take her to the nurse's office," he said in a commanding voice.

Emma gently lifted Valarie to her feet and helped her down the hall. Her head was still spinning. She looked back at David one last time to see tears welling up in his eyes.

"I'm sorry," he mouthed.

Valarie turned away. Her lungs felt tight and she would have given anything for the strength to run away.

"Dad, please, it's okay." Valarie sat on the hard chairs outside the principal's office, holding an ice pack to her face. Emma had helped her make it to the nurse's office and within a half hour her dad showed up in a furious rage that Valarie had never witnessed before. With both hands on his hips, he paced the hallway, waiting for Eric's parents to come out so he could declare that he was going to press charges against the boy for hitting his daughter.

"No, it's not okay, Valarie, this boy hit you and he will be punished."

"He didn't mean to hit me on purpose...I got in the way."

Her dad stopped pacing the hallway and faced her. She could tell he was waiting for further explanation.

"I tried to separate the fight," Valarie confessed, looking down at her shoes.

Tom's arms dropped to his sides. "What did you do that for?"

Valarie tried to blink back tears. She could see Eric's hands around David's throat, and the fearful look on his face, as if he was afraid the kid was going to suffocate him to death. She felt stupid for trying to separate them, but she didn't want David to get hurt. She waited for her dad to start lecturing her on the foolishness of her actions. Tears spilled over her still swollen eyes as the scene kept replaying itself in her head. Then she saw David hit Eric with enough force to break his nose.

"Well?" her dad asked, waiting for an answer.

"Because I was afraid he was going to kill David," she said, in a voice louder than one she intended to speak with.

Her dad's face softened as he heard her shout. Valarie turned her face away again, this time ashamed of yelling at her dad. She heard him sigh then she heard his footsteps grow closer. She felt a hand on her knee and saw him at eye level as he kneeled down to face her. She set the ice pack on the seat next to her and looked at him with watery eyes. His face grimaced as he saw the damage.

"Wait till you see what David did to the other kid," she said, trying to lighten the mood.

Her dad shook her head, as if he didn't know what to say. "You should have just let them fight it out," he finally said.

Valarie's eyes dropped from his gaze. "I know. I was just scared for David. I didn't want him to get hurt."

"I know, Val." He let out a long sigh. "When the one you care about is in trouble you will do anything for them, even if that means taking a blow for them."

Valarie's eyes began to sting from the tears. *Don't deny it,* her mind told her, *you did it because you love him, otherwise you would have let the two duke it out.* She nodded, as if she was agreeing with herself.

The door to the office opened. Eric's mother came out, followed by Eric. Tom paused as he saw the kid's swollen and busted face. The boy's eyes traveled to his feet as if he felt ashamed for what had happened. Valarie was glad that he felt ashamed. She wanted to charge at him and hit him back. It took everything in her to stay in her seat.

"Is there something you want to say?" his mother asked in a cold told of voice.

Eric lifted his head and fixed his gaze on Valarie. His swollen eyes looked narrow and hateful. She wondered if he was angry at her. "Sorry," he said.

"Go to the car," his mother demanded, and she watched as her son walked down the hallway and out of sight. She looked at Tom and opened her mouth to speak. At a loss for words, she let out a sigh.

"Don't worry about it," Tom said, waving his hand. He didn't sound as furious as he was a moment before. "Whatever punishment he got here is enough. Besides, I'm sure that face hurts like no other."

Eric's mother seemed shocked, yet relieved. "I'm just sorry she got in the middle of it," she said, waving a hand toward Valarie. She sounded sincere in her apology, but Valarie was sorry for her. She saw frustration in the woman's eyes, and wondered if her son had always caused trouble. Valarie would hate to live with someone like Eric.

The woman sighed again. "Thank you for not pressing charges."

"Not this time," he said. His voice sounded like a warning.

The woman nodded then without another word she followed her son down the hall.

"Mr. Edwards, will you step inside please." Valarie heard the principal call for her father. She stood and picked up her ice pack.

"I'll go sit in the truck," she said. Her dad handed her his keys, and disappeared into the office. She made her way out of the school and outside before she heard her name behind her. She knew who was calling her, but her feet kept moving.

"Valarie," David called for a third time.

This time Valarie stopped. She turned around to face him, glaring at him through angry tears. His face was a mixture of red and purple color, and there was crookedness to his nose that wasn't there the night before. He slowly approached her as if he was creeping up on a ticking time bomb. He stopped once he was a foot away. His eyes were fixed on her injury, and Valarie saw a flash of anger in his own eyes.

"It will heal," she said. Her voice was flat. "You've got bigger things to worry about than me."

"Don't say that," David said. "If I didn't care about you I wouldn't have beaten his butt."

"What is that supposed to mean?" she asked, wondering if he was blaming her for the beating.

David turned away.

"What happened?" she asked.

David shook his head. "He said something about you that he shouldn't have."

"What did he say?"

"It doesn't matter. What matters is he should've gotten a more severe punishment than just suspension."

"Eric was expelled?" Valarie asked in surprise.

David nodded. "He started it. He slammed me into the locker. I only hit him to make him let go of me. I was acting in self-defense." He paused before he added, "Apparently this isn't the first fight he's caused."

"What about the beating you gave him?" Valarie asked.

David shrugged his shoulders. "It was only worth a month of detention."

Valarie tried to process what he was telling her. "So… you stood up for me?" she asked, wondering if she was hallucinating from her injury.

"Yes."

"Why?" she asked. *Why else?* her mind told her. *You know why.*

David hesitated, "Because," he paused, as if he was trying to push the words out. "Because I love you, Valarie. And when he said all those hateful words it just made me so angry that I could have…" His voice trailed off, but Valarie didn't need to hear anymore. She felt the tears slowly roll down her face. She was afraid he would say those three words, yet at the same time, she hoped he would. He took a beating for her. How could she repay that? She looked down at her feet. Then she took his hand and gave him the ice pack. "You need it more than I do."

David laughed. "Thanks."

Valarie looked up into his eyes. They didn't look cloudy anymore, and she thought she caught a glimpse of a sparkle. She heard the sound of footsteps nearby and looked up from her hand to see her dad approaching. He stopped next to David and examined his face.

"I'm sorry Valarie got hurt, sir," David said, trying to face the man. "It was my fault."

Tom looked at Valarie then back at David. Without saying anything, he held out his hand. Valarie watched as David hesitated. He must have been expecting her dad to start yelling at him. He slowly shook her dad's hand.

"You shouldn't have beaten him so hard, you know," Tom said.

David nodded. "Yes, sir. If I may say so, I'm not proud of myself right now."

Tom nodded, as if he agreed that David should be ashamed of himself. "I have to thank you."

"Why, sir?" David asked with a surprised look on his swollen face.

"You stood up for my daughter."

Valarie's heart sank at her father's words. He almost sounded as if she was worthy of someone getting beat up for. She tried to push back a sob.

David nodded again. "You're welcome."

Tom sighed. "I'll be in the truck," he told Valarie then walked away. She could tell he was upset. She looked at David. Besides the swelling, his face looked sad. She grew angry with herself for trying to break up a fight between two teenage boys. She should have gotten the principal or a teacher instead. *Now your boyfriend is in trouble*, her mind told her, *it's your fault he got hit in the first place*. She shook her head at herself, trying to push back the tears. Her body felt tired after the excitement and her head was throbbing. All she wanted was to go home and hide under her bedcovers for a week. *He did it for you*, her mind continued, *because he loves you. Do it, girl, do it*, her mind told her. Summoning all the strength she had, she pushed back her tears and swung her arms around David's neck. "I love you too," she whispered in his ear. She felt his arms encircle her small torso. She stood there holding him for what felt to her was only a few seconds. Then she let go of him and ran to her father's truck, leaving him alone on the sidewalk. She wiped her face after she buckled her seat belt. She heard her father sigh.

"Val," he said. His voice was serious. "I'm going to ask you a question, and I want you to be honest. Don't worry about upsetting me with your answer, just be honest."

Valarie braced herself.

"What does David mean to you?"

Valarie felt the hot tears continue to flow. There was no point in stopping them now. She looked at her dad to see him staring back at her. "I think I love him, Dad," she said in a quiet voice.

Her dad nodded, as if he was trying to process her words. "Okay," he said. He looked out the windshield.

Valarie waited for him to start a lecture about how much of a bad influence David was, and why she shouldn't be with him, but instead he remained quiet.

"So," he said with a sigh. "The kid who hit you was expelled today, David gets a month's detention, and you've got a beat up face."

"I'm sorry," Valarie said.

Her dad was silent for a few minutes then he said, "I just don't want to be called into the principal's office every day."

Valarie shook her head. "You won't. I promise."

Her dad sighed again. "You're not in trouble this time. But if another fight breaks out, go get an adult, don't try to break it up."

Valarie nodded again, letting her dad know that she understood him.

"Okay," he said. He started the truck. "Let's get you home."

CHAPTER 15

Valarie wasn't sure what to do with herself for the rest of the day. She had never been pulled out of school before, and staying at home while her classes were going on without her gave her a feeling that her world was out of balance. Her father let out a heavy sigh as soon as he walked through the front door.

"Well," he said, setting his keys on the coffee table. "Since neither of us have plans anymore, why don't we go check out the peach trees?" He looked at Valarie and gave her a gentle smile. Valarie tried to smile back, but she didn't put much effort into looking happy. She followed her dad outside and into the orchard. Even though she was amongst the trees almost every night, she hadn't stopped to examine them in a while. Spring was nearing its end and summer sunshine was starting to touch the trees. They had already begun to bud and bloom. She had even found a small peach no bigger than the size of a quarter. Valarie could smell its sweetness and it gave her a sudden urge to sink her teeth into a juicy, ripe peach. She watched as her father touched the tiny fruit, examined its skin, the leaves, even the branches and the trunk. He sure went all in when he "checked out" the orchard.

"This was your mother's favorite time of year," he said, his back was turned away from her. "I remember when you were a baby, she carried you out here every time we came to look them over, and one time, just when your teeth were coming in and you could eat solid foods, she gave you a peach the size of your head, and the look on your face was like it was Christmas. You smiled so big and looked so happy to have been given a peach all of your own."

Valarie listened and tried to imagine herself as a baby in her mother's arms. Her father turned toward her and was silent for a while before he spoke. "I think I missed something along the way, Val."

"What do you mean?" she asked, taking a step closer to him.

"You're all grown up. I don't know when that happened."

Valarie didn't know what to say. Was he sad that she had grown up? She didn't feel grown up. Maturity and responsibility meant nothing to her if she was too shy and quiet to associate with people. Sometime she still wanted to hide behind her dad whenever someone tried to talk to her.

"I wish I could go back to be being a kid," she confessed.

Her father almost laughed. "No, don't do that. You've come too far and learned too much to start over."

"Life is too hard as a grownup," Valarie said.

Her father nodded as if he agreed. "Life is hard. But you can't escape it. You got to live through it and embrace whatever happens. There is a reason for everything, my dear."

"I wish I knew the reasons for everything," she said.

"I do too. But we don't, and there's no point in trying to figure out what were not supposed to know."

Valarie looked down at her shoes and kicked at the dirt. She wished she knew why God hadn't let her mother live, and why David had suffered the way he had. But she had the feeling that she may never know the reason for either of those.

"I've been trying to do the best I can for you ever since your mom died," her dad said. "But I feel like it's not enough."

Valarie faced her father. "It's more than enough," she said in a defensive sort of voice. She didn't want her dad to look down on himself. "You two gave me everything you could, I don't need anything else."

Her father was silent, as if he was thinking, then he said, "It's my job to protect you…and I've failed you today."

Valarie felt her heart break. She walked up to her dad and wrapped her arms around his waist. "You're not a failure. And it wasn't your fault," she said. Her father hugged her back, and Valarie felt his strong arms cover her.

She remembered telling David the same words the night before. She wondered when the guilty feelings were going to end.

"David has changed you, you know," her father said.

Valarie pulled away enough to face him. "What do you mean?"

Her father's eyes glistened, as if he was fighting back tears. "You're different."

"How so?"

"You're more outspoken than you were a few months ago. It's like he's brought you out of your shell and helped you open your eyes."

Valarie knew he was right. She felt different, almost braver and less afraid. She wondered how one person could bring such change into her life.

"I'll have to thank him for that too," her father said, holding her close again.

The day after the fight, Valarie found David waiting for her where her father dropped her off outside the school. She walked up to him and tried to smile. Without saying a word, he took her hand. Valarie saw a look of contentment in his still swollen eyes. The two walked inside the school hand in hand for the first time. Right away she noticed kids glancing at them and whispering to each other as they passed by in the halls. It was harder than usual for her to avoid eye contact with everyone. The students were watching her as if she had stepped out on stage. In her classes without David, some of the kids asked her if she was all right and few asked her why she tried to break up the fight. She told them she didn't want to see David get hurt, and when she was asked if she and David were "together," she would nod and say yes. Some of the kids looked as if they didn't believe her, others looked surprised. She could hear what they were thinking as if they were speaking their thoughts. *How did Miss Invisible get a cool guy like David?* Her mind asked her the same question. She tried to shake it off. She was glad when school was over and her father came to take her home, yet at the same time she felt bad for leaving David at the school while he served his detention.

"Don't worry," he told her the first day of his punishment, "I survived a three-day stomach bug once. I can survive this."

Valarie smiled. She hugged him tight before he disappeared into the detention room. She wondered if it was scary in there, like the dark forest from the fairy tales her mother read to her as a child. She thought about how much she missed her mom. She would give anything for her to be there during such a confusing time in her life.

That night, Valarie took her usual walk out to the corner of the peach orchard. The sky was clear and the air was a bit too warm for her skin. She could hear the crickets chirping, as if they were having some kind of conversation.

She stopped at the tree that David had punched. As she stared at it, she noticed that a small piece of its bark was missing. She knew he must have broken something.

"When will the peaches be ready to eat?" David asked, approaching her with his flashlight.

"Not for another month or two. They're not big enough."

David stopped near the tree. "That's too bad, I could really go for a peach smoothie right now."

Valarie turned to him. His face looked less painful in the dark. "How are you feeling?"

He shrugged. "I'm okay. How is your eye?"

"It's fine," she said. She didn't think it was a big deal.

David turned off his flashlight. He stepped closer to her and for the first time Valarie took his hand. She looked up at his face to see a bright red color appear on his cheekbones, a color she knew was not caused by the bruising. She couldn't help but smile at him.

"I have something for you," he said. He handed her a small rectangular object. David turned his flashlight back on to reveal a picture frame. It was the photo from his spring formal, the one that was taken as the two entered the gym. Valarie saw the smile on her face as she posed for the photo. *I look happy*, she thought. She remembered the nervousness she felt that night, especially when he slipped his arm around her. Then she remembered the kiss that she had interrupted. She looked at David. Even though his face was beat up, he was still the most handsome boy she had ever met.

"It's a great picture, huh?" David said.

Valarie nodded. She couldn't seem to take her eyes away from him. She felt hot on the inside, and a strange tingling sensation flowed through her arms. She wasn't sure what she was feeling, but she knew that she was filled with a whole new admiration for him.

"You look happy, Valarie," he said, as if he had read her mind. "When we first met I thought your face was broken because you never smiled."

"It was broken," Valarie said sarcastically. "But you fixed it."

He cleared his throat. "I like seeing you smile. It's beautiful."

Valarie bit her lip, trying not to blush.

"My parents say we make a great couple."

"My dad say's you've brought me out of my shell," she said, as if they were taking turns confessing what their elders were saying.

"We make a good pair, don't you think?"

"We make a weird pair."

The expression in his face changed and he became serious. "Maybe we're meant to be."

Valarie didn't know what to say. Her whole life had been turning upside down for months, she wasn't sure of anything anymore.

With his other free hand, David gently touched her face near her swollen eye then he leaned forward and gently pressed his lips against her wounded skin. Valarie felt tingling run through her body, and her heart seemed to have stopped. She could feel the warmth of his breath on her face as he sighed.

"I'm sorry," he said, pulling himself away. "I promised I wouldn't do that."

She shook her head. "It's all right," she said, not knowing what else to say. She tried to breath in deep to prevent her lungs from growing tight. She stared at David for a while, resisting the urge to wrap her arms around him and kiss him. She didn't know what she was waiting for, but she knew that she didn't want to do it just yet.

"Thanks for the picture," she said, trying to break the awkward silence.

"You're welcome." His voice was soft. Valarie wondered if he felt embarrassed.

"How was detention?" she asked.

David shrugged his shoulders. "Not too bad. Just sat at a desk and minded my own business for four hours."

"Do your parents hate me now?" She looked down at her shoes.

"No. They know it wasn't your fault."

"It was my fault," she protested. "It all started because he made a comment about me."

"Just because he said something about you doesn't make it your fault. It was his fault for saying it in the first place."

Valarie faced him. "Am I ever going to know what he said?"

It was David's turn to look down. "It doesn't matter, it's all over now."

"Why won't you tell me?"

"You don't need to know."

Valarie sighed. "Isn't communication the number one thing in a relationship?"

A smile stretched across David's face as he heard the words he spoke to her not three days ago. "He said…" David hesitated and bit his lip. "He told me to leave you alone if I already got what I wanted from you."

Valarie studied his face. "What is that supposed to mean?"

"It means he assumed I would take advantage of you. And if I had, then there was no other reason for me to be with you."

Valarie looked back down at her shoes. She suddenly felt exposed, and at the same time she felt angry with Eric all over again. The stupid kid didn't even know her, and he was making jokes like that? What else had he said about her?

"After he said that I told him to shut up," David continued. "And when he said he was only joking I told him to not joke that way. Then he got defensive and when I tried to walk away he pushed me. I fell to the floor and as soon as I got up he hit me. I hit him back before he pinned me to the locker then I hit him again to make him release me. That's when you came in."

"Why would he think something like that?" she asked. She immediately regretted the question.

"I don't know. Because he's stupid and assumed that I was a woman user." David sighed. "I think he's jealous."

"Why would he be jealous?"

"After what he did at the dance, I wouldn't put it past him." She felt David squeeze her hand as she tried to remember exactly what happened at the formal. Eric had approached her and told her that she looked good. He had looked her up and down, making her feel exposed. She shivered.

"Val," David said. "Please look at me." She hesitated then looked at him anyway. She saw in his eyes the same intense honesty she had seen that night at the diner.

"I want you to know that I won't do that to you. I'm not that kind of guy, and I'd rather die than use a girl for physical pleasure or lead her to believe that I love her if I didn't. You know that, right?"

Valarie nodded. She believed him.

David sighed. "I will protect you from him."

"Look where that's got you."

"Well, it's his own fault for starting the fight," he said. "I love you, and love always protects." He leaned his forehead against hers and gently whispered, "I won't let you go unless you want me to."

Valarie felt her face grow hot. She looked down at her hand in his and breathed in deep.

"This relationship stuff is complicated," she said. Her heart felt heavy with all that had gone on over the past few days.

David gave her hand a gentle squeeze. "It's worth it," he said. "You're worth it."

Valarie knew there was no point in arguing with him. She had learned that he was stubborn when it came to caring for people. She was used to everyone leaving her alone and now that he loved her and wanted to defend her, she didn't know what to do.

"Valarie?" His voice was soft.

She looked at him.

"Would you like to come to church with me this Sunday?"

Valarie thought the conversation couldn't get any more difficult, now he was asking her to go to church.

She shook her head. "I don't know, David. I don't really believe in that stuff."

"I know. But I figured after what we've been through, you could use some comfort."

"I don't find comfort in God."

David shrugged his shoulders. "Maybe it's time you did."

CHAPTER 16

Valarie hadn't been to church for almost a year. She enjoyed going with her parents, when her mother asked for them to join her, but after her mother grew weak and couldn't go anymore, the visits stopped altogether. After her mother died her father didn't go back, nor did he ask Valarie if she wanted to go. She could remember the first time her mother asked them to go with her one August morning. Valarie's father laughed. Then he saw that his wife was serious, and he agreed to go to please her. She wondered if he liked it at all, but she gave him credit for going to make his wife happy.

Valarie sighed heavily. The minutes on her clock slowly passing by. It was now after two a.m. She had been lying in bed for almost two hours, listening to the crickets chirping. The sound was beginning to irritate her. Or maybe it was just the thoughts that were driving her insane. She didn't want to walk into a church and put a fake smile on her face so no one would think she was depressed. She didn't want to be around happy people when her world was crumbling down upon her. But David was right, she could use some comfort, and she remembered walking away with a happy feeling after service. But this time would be different. God had taken away her mother and David's first girlfriend. There was no point in faking her beliefs. She rolled over to her left side, trying to clear her mind long enough to fall asleep.

Why had God taken away her mother, even though she asked Him not to? Wasn't He kind, loving, and giving, wasn't that what she had learned in church? She had begged for God to spare her mother's life like a child would plead for a piece of candy. But God didn't hear her, or maybe He did and only ignored her plea. But God didn't ignore His children, she had learned that too. So why did God take her mother away? All she wanted was a reason. Maybe if she knew the reason, she would be able to believe in Him. She sat up in bed. The crickets seemed to have grown louder, like they were all screaming at once. She stood and went over to her desk. She looked down at the picture of her and David. Both their faces looked as if they had never suffered any loss. Why had God taken away Mandy too? Didn't He know that David was trying to help her? Couldn't God have encouraged him and opened Mandy's eyes to see that she needed help? Why did God ignore their cries? Did He only listen to adults and not teenagers? Where they not old or mature enough? Was there some kind of rulebook to talking with God?

Valarie turned away and went over to her door mirror. She looked at herself. Even in the dark she could see the mark Eric left on her face. Every time she looked at it, she felt like she hated that kid more and more. She gently touched the wound, and for a second her feelings changed. She felt David's fingers on her skin and his lips touch her. She had wanted to kiss him, but something held her back, something she could not explain. She sighed aloud and sat on the side of her bed. Too many things happened in her life that she couldn't explain. She was tired of events taking place without reason. Why couldn't she just know the answers to her questions? She took a pillow from the head of her bed and hugged it. She heard the crickets calling out and put the pillow over her head to cover her ears. It didn't drown out the noise. Why had God taken away her mother? Why had God let Mandy kill herself? Why didn't God hear her and David? Why couldn't she have the reasons why? Why? Why? Why?

Valarie took the pillow, buried her face in the cotton and screamed. She screamed long and hard until she couldn't breathe. She pulled the pillow away from her face and took a deep breath in. Then she slammed her head back into the pillow and screamed again. She screamed until she couldn't scream anymore. Then she began to sob. There were too many questions that she didn't have the answers to.

"There's no point in trying to figure out what we're not supposed to know," her father had said. Valarie wasn't sure if she could accept that. She wanted to know, she needed to know, didn't she? She cried into her pillow until her fingertips began to feel numb from lack of oxygen. She lifted her head and threw the pillow back on the bed.

"Okay," she said aloud, as if she was admitting defeat. She looked up to the ceiling of her attic and wondered if God was watching her. "I don't need the reasons," she said. "Just take away the pain."

"You will?" David asked, a look of surprise painted across his face.

Valarie set her water cup down on the cafeteria table, trying to ignore the headache she had been fighting since her breakdown the night before. She couldn't bring herself to eat anything, yet she felt an unquenchable thirst. She knew she was getting dehydrated from all the crying she had done over the past few days.

"I will."

David looked at his tray. He hadn't been able to eat anything either. Valarie guessed that she and David were under too much stress to be busy consuming food. "Are you sure you want to go with me? I mean, I know how you feel about church," he said, facing her.

"What else have I got to lose?" she asked, sounding less than enthused.

David smiled.

On the truck ride home, Valarie had announced that she wanted to go to church with David that coming Sunday. Her father gave her the same look of surprise that David had shown at lunch.

"Really?" he asked.

"Yes."

Her father was quiet then he said, "This isn't peer pressure, is it?"

Valarie smiled. "No," she said. "It's more of a teenage crisis."

David picked her up in his father's car around nine Sunday morning. Valarie had been awake since six, unable to fall back to sleep. She dressed herself in a nice blouse and her only pair of blue jeans that didn't have holes. She tried to cover her wound with makeup, and put a pink headband in her hair. She didn't know when she started to care about how she looked. Maybe David had changed that too. Her father had joked with her to be good in church, and she gave him a hug before she left saying that he wouldn't get called into the pastor's office. She shut the front door behind her just as David got out of the car to open the passenger door. She noticed that he had dressed a little nicer than usual as well and she couldn't help but smile to herself as she got into the car. Then the two drove out of the driveway and down the long empty road.

"How are you this morning?" he asked her, looking at her then the road.

"I'm fine. How are you?" she asked. She didn't want to let him know that she had been up half the night fighting her thoughts yet again.

"I'm good," he said honestly. Valarie was almost jealous.

"Do your parents go to church?"

David nodded. "Usually, but my mom has one of her headaches this morning, so she stayed home today. My dad always stays with her when she's not feeling good."

Valarie nodded. She looked out the window at the passing trees and breathed in deep. She didn't know what she was expecting to find at church, but she hoped it would be some form of relief from her emotions. They drove for about a half hour before pulling into the parking lot of a small red brick building. Valarie expected white walls and a four-foot steeple sitting on the roof, but the building looked no different than a business office or small school. She wondered how many times she had passed by and never noticed it was sitting there. David drove up and down a few rows of cars before he found an empty spot. He hurried to open her door.

"Are you ready?" he asked, taking her hand.

She nodded, even though her stomach was in a knot. Once inside, Valarie saw many people of all ages. She thought of the Sunday mornings at her mother's church and felt a sudden longing for her mother's embrace. People were talking with each other; some were laughing and some were listening. A little girl was showing her friend her dress while a little boy was playing with his toy car. Older gentlemen in suits were grouped together like a pack of cheerleaders, and Valarie noticed that most of the adults were holding Styrofoam cups, filled with coffee, no doubt. The foyer was small, but elegant with flowers and a few small wooden tables for the elderly to sit. The carpet was an ugly grey and the walls were white, but despite the bleak appearance, the people looked happy, as if they didn't have a care in the word. She suddenly regretted walking through the doors.

David waved and said hello to many people both old and young. Some stopped and asked who "this nice young lady" was, and David introduced her as his girlfriend. They shook her hand, said it was nice to meet her then they went on their way. A gentleman in a navy suit with combed gray hair shook her hand with much enthusiasm, too much she thought. David had whispered to her that he was the Pastor. He then led her into the sanctuary where she caught sight of several long wooden pews covered with red velvet. On the grey carpet stage were a drum set, three guitars and a few microphones, along with more flowers and even candles. Valarie saw a screen on the wall behind the stage project good morning greetings. She wished she was as happy as the people looked. David led her to a pew not far from the back.

"My parents and I usually sit here," he said.

She sat on the soft velvet and continued to observe people as they made their way into the sanctuary. Across the aisle, she saw three small girls sitting in a row and as she looked closer she realized that they were triplets. One was flipping through her Bible; the other two were talking with each other. A man Valarie assumed was their father was on his feet talking with another grey-haired gentleman. She wondered how the man could have such well-behaved children.

A moment later a woman walked up on the stage and greeted the congregation. Others followed her, taking their places among the instruments. Music started playing and David stood. Valarie stood with him as people started singing. She felt out of place not knowing the lyrics, but she listened to David as he sang with a strong sturdy voice. She had never heard him sing before. His voice was pleasant her. He turned to face her then he took her hand again. He stopped singing long enough to smile then he turned back to the screen and continued to sing. Valarie saw the lyrics running on the screen, but she didn't bother singing along. She didn't know the rhythm. The upbeat music lasted through three songs before it slowed down. Valarie couldn't help but feel as if she had heard the song before; it must have been played at her mother's church once or twice. Then she remembered where she had heard it. Her mother used to sing the song while she cooked or cleaned the house. She said it was her favorite, and Valarie would sit outside the kitchen just to listen to her sing. Tears began to sting her eyes. *No, not right now*, she thought. She didn't want to cry anymore. She was glad when the song was over and the pastor walked onto the stage and asked for everyone to be seated. As she sat, she wiped her eyes and wondered how she was going to sit through an hour of preaching. *It's bad enough that you have to sit through eight hours of school five days a week*, she thought. *When did you get so cranky?* her mind asked. *Since my life started to fall apart*, she answered.

She watched the pastor as he opened his Bible and began to read from one of the gospels, something about a blind man who was a beggar, and when heard that Jesus was nearby he started crying out to Him for healing. *Yeah, you're not the only one*, Valarie thought.

"And the people nearby were telling him to be quiet," the pastor said, looking up from his Bible. "They were more than likely thinking that Jesus was too important to associate with a bling beggar. But this beggar, persistent and desperate for Jesus's healing, kept calling for Him. He wanted Jesus's healing, he needed Jesus's healing, it was so close he could practically taste it." *So close*, Valarie thought. Tears threatened to fill her eyes again, and she forced them away.

"So Jesus told His disciples to help the blind man to Him," the pastor continued. "And when the blind man reached Him, He asked, 'What do you want me to do for you?' Isn't that a funny question? The Son of God, who knows all things and is all things good, asks this blind beggar what he wants from God. Why do you think that is?" He was silent for a moment, as if giving the congregation some time to think. "Maybe God wanted him to ask healing. Maybe God wanted the blind man to ask for himself instead of just saying, 'You know what I want.' God wanted him to ask. His word says, 'Ask and it shall be given unto you.' Too many times do we assume that God knows what we want, and while it is true that He knows what we want, He also wants us to come to Him, and humbly ask for what it is that we need."

I have asked, Valarie thought. *God just isn't listening to me.*

"And God answers us," the pastor continued. "We may not think He answers us or feel His answer, but He does answer. He answers us in forms of a yes, no, or not yet. Many times we are so consumed in what we want and what it is that we've asked Him for that we don't hear His answer. We when ask we have to stop," he paused for a second, "listen," he put his hand to his ear, "and receive what God is telling us whether it's what we want to hear or not. But God doesn't answer on your timing, no, He answers when His time is right, and so when the beggar asked for sight, Jesus healed him, making his eyes like new, and the beggar saw the world around him. God knows what we need before we ask Him, yet He calls us to ask. And when we don't always get the answer we want, that doesn't mean that we didn't get any answer. That just means that we got His answer instead of what we wanted. We got what He planned and what He knows we need."

Valarie looked down at her lap, feeling like a scolded child. She had asked God for answers, but she didn't listen for them. She asked assuming that she would get what she asked for, and when she didn't get a response, she gave up. Her heart broke as the pastor's words rolled over in her head. *Okay*, she told God, *I hear you now. I hear you speaking to me through this man.* She looked back up at the pastor and continued to listen.

"And when we don't get the answer we want, we get upset with life," the pastor was saying. "We get upset and angry with our circumstances and with those around us. We are human, we are selfish, and we will fail. But God won't fail. And he doesn't push us away either. We can come to Him and ask for forgiveness, and you know what? He'll forgive you."

Valarie felt a tear roll down her face. *God*, she prayed, *I'm sorry.* She sniffed and David turned to her. He glimpsed at her face and looked concerned. Valarie waved her hand, letting him know that he didn't have to worry about her.

"Are you all right, Valarie? You were tearing up in there." David had driven the car out of the parking lot before he asked her the question. Church had passed slowly, but

Valarie had taken in every word the pastor spoke, and she tried to remember where in the Bible the pastor had spoken from, she wanted to read it when she got home. She was sure her dad had kept her mother's Bible somewhere.

"Yeah, I'm okay." Her eyes burned as she blinked, and her nose was congested, but for the first time in a long time she felt all right. Her heart felt lighter and her spirit wasn't so broken any more.

"What brought you to tears?" he asked, taking her hand and keeping the other on the steering wheel.

"What pastor had said about telling God what you need. It makes me wonder if I've been coming to him all wrong."

David almost laughed. "There's no wrong or right way to talk to God, Valarie. Just go to him, tell him what you need, and let him take care of the rest."

Valarie was silent for a moment then she asked, "How do you believe in God after all that has happened to you?"

It was David's turn to be silent. He seemed to be thinking and Valarie wondered if he was going to respond at all. "Walking in faith is no picnic, Valarie. It's not a magical life where you dance in the sunshine and get what you want when you want. It's a hard road, a narrow road, but God doesn't leave you alone to fend for yourself. He helps in ways that you may never know; a miracle, big or small, an act of kindness from someone. There's a popular saying that God works in mysterious ways, but personally I think that's way underestimated."

"Why is it underestimated?"

"Because God's works are too awesome for us to understand, that's why it's mysterious. People think that God will grant them anything when the truth is we have to learn and grow and seek Him. Sometimes we simply have to follow Him blindly; it's called walking by faith. We got to trust that God knows what He's doing and continue on with our life. I know there was a reason for loosing Mandy, and even though I don't know what that reason is, I have to trust that God knows what He is doing, and that I got to let Him roll out my life. And I'll tell you right now, that choice was the hardest choice I've ever had to make."

Valarie nodded. She was beginning to agree.

CHAPTER 17

The last day of school for the seniors came all too soon for Valarie. David's last day passed by like any other day, and when school was out, all the seniors rushed outside, throwing papers and books with excitement. Valarie wondered if they all had to go back and pick them up later.

David had taken her to church with him and his parents every Sunday since she had first went with him. It was a little awkward having his parents with them, but whenever they spoke to people and sat to listen to the pastor, Valarie could tell that they were a true family, and that they loved each other very much. There were a few Sundays when Valarie asked her dad if he would like to go with them, but he would shake his head, thank her, and tell her no. He always told her to have fun. Now with David free of school, she would go back to being alone during her classes and at lunchtime. She would only be able to see David at night when they walked the orchard and on Sundays. She felt as if their time together was getting cut short. But she was determined to include David in her life as usual and to release her prideful assumptions of her future to God. Late one night, before she had gone outside to meet David, she had sat on her bed for what felt like hours, and she whispered two simple words that seemed to change her life. She said, "I'm sorry." She let go of trying to find the answers to why she and David had suffered such loss, and she tried to be honest with God, no matter how weird it made her feel. She still hadn't gotten used to talking aloud with no physical being to listen. But soon she found herself talking and not caring who was around.

The night of the last day of school, Valarie and David walked the orchard hand in hand. Both were quiet for a long time and Valarie fixed her focus on the peaches. The fruit was turning red and orange and smelling sweeter than ever.

"Aren't they ready to eat yet?" he asked, almost like a whining child.

Valarie smiled. "Almost," she said.

The two were silent again then he spoke. "I want to go somewhere tomorrow, just the two of us, before all the chaos of graduation hits me."

"Where would you like to go?"

"I don't know, but we haven't really been on a date yet, except for the dance."

Valarie had to think...he was right. "Surprise me," she said.

David stopped walking. He smiled at her. "All right," he said then he continued to walk.

Valarie felt as if she had just signed her life away. Knowing David he would probably sign her up to bungee jump off a bridge. She let out a deep sigh. "Everything keeps changing on me. Life won't stay still long enough for me to catch up."

David nodded. "You've come a long way since I've known you."

"I'm going to be alone at school now," she said in a tone of disappointment.

"It's only for a little while. This time next year, you'll be a free bird too."

"I won't know what to do with myself then," she confessed.

"Well, I remember you telling me you want to go to college. So study hard and start thinking about where and what you want to study."

Valarie didn't want to think about that. She just wanted to enjoy the moments she had with David. "I'm going to miss you," she said.

David stopped again and looked her in the eyes. "I'm not going anywhere. I'll be here when you come out of your house at the end of the day. Speaking of that, how long has it been since you did one of your mad dashes into the orchard?"

Valarie smiled. "Three weeks, and counting." David gazed at Valarie with a content sort of look on his face. "Good," he said. "That makes me happy."

"I have you to thank, David."

A sudden rush of color appeared on his cheeks and he tried to hide a smile.

"What is it?" she asked, concerned that she had embarrassed him. He shook his head.

"I just like when you say my name, is all."

It was Valarie's turn to blush.

"I love you, Valarie." Her face grew hot, and she was sure her skin was red. David let out a laugh. "You're glowing like a Christmas tree," he said.

Valarie laughed. It was his entire fault that she blushed, but for the first time it was okay. The heat in her face seemed to increase as he began to stroke her hair. His fingers ran over the area under her eye that had scared. "I love you," he said in a more sincere tone of voice.

Valarie stared into his eyes as if she was seeing them for the first time. She saw his love for her. She saw that it was deep and wide.

"How did someone like you come my way?" she asked, as if she was talking to herself.

David shrugged his shoulders, still stroking her hair. "God works in mysterious ways." His voice was still soft.

Valarie felt as if her heart was trying to beat its way out of her chest.

"May I ask you something, Valarie?"

"Anything," she said, almost feeling mesmerized.

"May I have your permission to kiss you?"

She swallowed hard as her lungs grew tight. The question made her nervous. She had forgotten that David said he would wait for her permission and now she wasn't sure what to say. She breathed in deep. "I've never kissed anyone before," she confessed.

"Neither have I," David said. He stopped stroking her hair and rested his fingers on her jawline.

"I don't know how," she said.

David smiled and his eyes sparkled. "I don't either," he said. He took a step closer. *What are you waiting for?* her mind asked her. *You know you want to. Then why am I afraid?* she asked herself. *Everyone is afraid at first,* her mind answered, *but there is nothing to be afraid of.*

Valarie took another deep breath then she nodded her head. "All right."

David smiled before he closed his eyes and began to lean toward her. She remembered the night he first tried to kiss her, and she hoped she wouldn't have a repeat of that. She closed her eyes and the next thing she felt was something warm and soft touching her lips. She quickly pulled away, and shivered.

"Are you all right?" David asked. His eyebrows were pulled together in confusion.

Valarie nodded. "I'm sorry," she said. She took a deep breath. "Can...can we try that again?"

David let out a laugh. "Sure."

Valarie closed her eyes again and waited for the same warm feeling to touch her, and when it did, she felt something like electricity flood onto her lips and down her arms. She stood still, not knowing if she should pucker up. She felt David's hand travel up her jaw and rest on the back of her neck. His hand was warm on her skin. She felt his lips pull away and she blinked her eyes open. She swallowed hard and was surprised to find that the lump in her throat was gone.

"Wow," she said softly, it was the first thing that came to her mind. David gently caressed her skin with his thumb. She looked up at him to see a new sparkle in his eyes, one that was brighter and more vivid. His face was full of red color and he acted as if he didn't know whether to smile or laugh.

With her eyes still on David, Valarie touched her lips and wondered if she had really been kissed.

"Are you all right?" David asked again. His voice was so soft it sounded hoarse.

Valarie nodded, unable to find her own voice. She felt David's hand pull away from her neck and she realized that he was still holding her other hand. She couldn't think, couldn't argue with herself, and couldn't feel upset. All she felt was loved, and it felt good.

David smiled at her. "I think we've had enough excitement for today. Let me get you home." He began to lead her back toward her house.

Valarie didn't know how her feet were still moving, but she walked to her front porch and stopped once she got to the first step. David turned to her and sighed. "You get some good rest, we have a date tomorrow."

She wasn't sure where her voice went, but she was still unable to speak. It almost made her feel frustrated. He gave her hand a gentle squeeze then gestured for her to go inside. She let go of him, climbed the steps like a slow moving cat. She paused as she reached for the doorknob. She turned back to him to see him still standing where she left him. He stared up at her with a look of admiration.

"Good night, beautiful," he said.

Valarie felt as if she was in a haze. Her mind was asleep and her bodily functions were just motions she was going through. She blinked her eyes, trying to bring herself back to reality. She suddenly wondered how David was still speaking, or how he was still standing.

"Good night," she said in a low tone of voice. She turned her back to him and reached for the door handle then on an impulse, she turned back to David, hastily walked down the front steps, and wrapped her arms around his neck. She looked up at him and gently put her lips to his. She felt his arms curl around her small torso and pull her close. Then she pulled away and leaned her head against his chest.

"I love you, David," she said. She faced him one more time before letting go. Then she walked back up the steps and went inside.

Valarie awoke the next morning to a ray of sunlight peeping in through her window. She was always up with the sun, this time the sun rose and watched over her for a while. She sat up and went over to her dresser and pulled out some clothes to wear. Then she went into the bathroom. She stopped as she looked into the mirror and saw herself. She leaned over the sink to get a closer look. Her skin had more color in it, and she thought her lips were a little bigger. Then she remembered what happened the night before. She touched her lips and smiled. She never knew that being kissed by someone who loved her would make her feel so special. She couldn't wait to see David again that day.

After she finished in the bathroom, she went downstairs and saw her dad in the kitchen standing over the stove.

"Hey, Val," he said. He turned around and smiled at her.

She took her usual seat at the table and cleared her throat. "Morning," she said, trying to suppress the smile that kept coming back.

"How are you?"

I'm great, Valarie thought, *I'm wonderful, I'm terrific, and I'm in love.* "I'm good," she said. "How are you?"

"So-so," he said. He stirred something in a pot then pulled out two bowls from the cupboard. "What's on your agenda for your first day of summer break?"

Valarie hadn't thought about it. What was she going to do? What would David be doing? Probably making plans for his graduation. Didn't he say he wanted to take her somewhere? She couldn't remember, the whole night felt like a blur. "I suppose I'll read something and just rest today," she answered. Her father turned the burner off and dished two bowls of steaming oatmeal. He placed on in front of her and handed her a spoon.

"Sound's good," he said. He set a bowl on his placemat and took his seat. "I'm going to be out today. It's time to gather my friends to go through the orchard and make plans for harvesting."

Valarie blew on her spoonful of oats. "Already?" she asked.

Her father nodded.

"Do you want me to go with you?" she asked.

"No, you've got your own plans," he said, as if he knew something she didn't. After they finished eating, her father put the dishes in the sink then took his phone and sat in the living room with his address book. Calling up his friends always took half a day. He spent hours talking with one friend about how the orchard was doing, what books he was reading, and how his other job was going. Valarie wondered if he felt lonely. She washed up the dishes and just as she sat down to read there was a knock on the door.

"Val, could you get that?" her dad asked as he was trying to dial a number with his large fingers.

Valarie went to the door and smiled when she saw David waiting for her on the other side.

"Hi," she said. Before another word was spoken, David took her in his arms and kissed her lightly. Then he released her and smiled. Valarie shook her head. She looked back to her father in the living room and saw that he was talking on the phone. She was glad he didn't witness the scene.

"What are you doing?" she asked David in a whisper.

"I've come to take you away," he whispered back.

"Where are we going?" she asked, still whispering.

"Someplace special."

Valarie looked back at her dad. "Just one second," she said. She approached her dad and waited for him to notice her presence.

"Hold on a second, Bobby. Yes, Val?" He looked up at her.

"May I go somewhere with David?" she asked. She held her hands behind her back like a little girl.

"Sure, just be home before dark please. All right, Bobby, what was I saying?"

Valarie left him to his conversation. She slipped on her shoes at the front door then left without another word. She saw that David had parked his dad's car in her driveway, and like always he opened her door for her.

"Where are we going?" she asked. She was barely able to contain her excitement. "Someplace special," he said again. He started the car and began to drive.

CHAPTER 18

Valarie was on pins and needles as David continued to drive. Into town and through the city streets he drove, not stopping for anything. She was beginning to wonder if he kidnapped her. After almost thirty minutes of driving, David pulled onto a dirt road and reduced his speed. He maneuvered the car with ease as if he had driven through dirt and rocks before. The road was bumpy, but soon he pulled off onto the grassy shoulder. Valarie looked around.

"Where are we?" she asked. She saw nothing but trees and grass.

"You'll see," David said. He unbuckled himself then got out and opened her door. He took her hand like he always did and lead her a few feet away from the car. "Watch your step," he warned. Valarie held his hand tight as he guided her through a wall of trees. It was like walking through a forest for Valarie. Fallen leaves and branches lay on the ground and a few thin trees had fallen over. After going through the wall David stopped. Valarie looked around her and saw that they had stepped into some sort of grove. Trees were swayed and bent to form an overhang while branches of all sizes closed them in like walls. In was dark and the air was cool. Grass grew richly on the ground, and logs lay scattered. It was beautiful to her.

David led her out into the middle of the grove and pulled out his phone. He began to play a song that Valarie recognized right away. He put his phone back in his pocket then he pulled her close to him and began to sway to the song they had danced to at his spring formal, the one she listened to everyday. She smiled wide as she moved with him. He leaned his forehead against hers and let out a sigh.

"How did I ever find you?" he asked. Valarie shrugged her shoulders.

"I don't know," she said. "But I'm glad you did."

"Me too," David said. "I hope we stay together."

"I hope so too," she said then it was her turn to sigh. "I'm already going crazy just thinking about school without you."

He gently lifted her chin and said, "I'll be there for you when the day is over." She nodded, letting him know that she understood. They continued to dance in each other's silent embrace, without a care of their future.

"Now where are we going?" Valarie asked, as David drove back toward town.

"I figured after our hiking this morning, you would be hungry."

At the mention of food her stomach growled, yet she felt too preoccupied to try to eat.

David reached over and took her hand. He smiled at her. Suddenly Valarie heard the sound of an approaching car. Her head was thrown forward and banged hard against the dashboard. She felt her world spin around her and then come to a sudden stop. Something soft yet firm hit her in the face. She didn't remember falling asleep, but she seemed to be dreaming as she found herself in a garden, a wide lovely garden with stone steps and flowers of all sorts of colors. She was sitting on a stone bench, as if waiting for somebody to meet her there. She looked down and noticed that the rich green grass was soft to her bare feet. The air was cool and crisp, feeling good to her lungs as she breathed in and out. Out of curiosity, she rose and began to walk the stone trail. The garden was empty, except for a few birds carrying out their daily business. Valarie wondered where she was, yet she had a strange feeling that she was all right. As she turned a corner hedge she saw a woman dressed completely in white standing still near a water fountain, staring at the stone as if she was in a trance. She was tall and thin, and long brown hair flowed down her back. The woman turned and faced Valarie, as if she felt her presence.

"Mama?" Valarie asked in disbelief.

Her mother smiled back at her with her wide smile and held out her arms. Valarie ran to her mother, nearly knocking her over when she threw her arms around her. She felt tears in her eyes, but they didn't sting like her tears usually did. Her mother's embrace was soft and warm, just like it had always been. She wondered if her mother had been in the garden ever since she had died. She felt her mother pull away and stare intently at her. Her brown eyes sparkled and her skin was glowing. She didn't speak, she only seemed happy to see her.

"I missed you," Valarie said.

Her mother smiled again. Valarie wondered if she had lost her voice. She saw a figure from behind her mother approach them, and Valarie looked to see who was coming.

"David?"

David stopped near her mother and smiled. He stuck his hands in the pockets of his beige slacks, and Valarie noticed that his hair was combed back and not one wrinkle was in his shirt. He seemed to have a different look in his eye, one of peace. Valarie held out his hand for him, and just as he reached for it, she felt a sharp pain in her left leg. The garden and her mother disappeared as Valarie's eyes shot open. Her first sight was a white cloth pressed against her face. It smelled like leather, and she tried to push it away. Her arms felt heavy as if they had been filled with rocks and it took much strength for her to lift her head. The white cloth she had seen was a bag. She wondered why the bag was shoved in her face. She noticed a wall of glass in front of her that was shattered yet still in one piece. Then she turned further left and saw a body-like shape with the same white bag. She blinked her eyes and tried to make sense of her surroundings.

She must have fallen asleep again, for the next thing she knew was that she was waking up a second time. Her mind seemed to be a little more alert and the pain in her leg caught her attention. She lifted her head again and looked around; the bag, the glass wall, the body. She tried to lean over but was held back by something on her chest; her seatbelt. She slowly unbuckled herself then leaned over and poked the shape. The shape didn't move. She poked it again. Nothing. She sat back in her seat and saw that the door to the passenger side was bent and squished, like a halfway crushed soda can. She pushed on it with her heavy arms, but it didn't budge. She pushed harder, and as she pushed she seemed to recollect the events that led up to that moment. She remembered that she and David were dancing in the trees then they were driving then she saw him and mother…but…her mother was dead, wasn't she? She pushed harder still. The door creaked as it began to budge. Why would she have seen her mother? Why couldn't her mother speak? Why couldn't David speak? How had he and her mother been in the same place at the same time? She pushed the door open just enough to squeeze out, but once she tried to move, that pain in her leg came back and she let out a cry. She felt hot tears rolling down her face. The realization came to her that her leg was more than likely broken. She squeezed her way through the gap and fell onto the ground. She crawled a few feet before rolling over onto her back. It took her a moment to come to her senses. She saw that the thing she had crawled out of was a car, and it was smashed into a large tree, almost wrapped around the trunk as if it was giving it a hug. When had she been in the car? It wasn't her dad's car...

She slowly pushed herself to her feet and limped over to the driver's side, crying as she went. The door was just as squished as the one she pushed open. She tried to pry it open, but it was a lot harder to pull on. Her arms just didn't have the strength. Who was in there anyway? Why was she even trying to get to them? She yanked as hard as she could, unable to get it open. She paused and looked around. Behind them, up on the road was a small truck, not nearly big enough to run them over. The front bumper was smashed and she thought she saw the same piece of shattered glass above the bumper. Had the truck run into them? Were they in an accident? She turned back to the door and tried to pull it again, this time it came a little more freely and when she got it open she saw that David was trying to unbuckle his belt. He turned to her with a hazy look in his eyes. He seemed to have fallen asleep too.

"Valarie?" he mumbled. His seatbelt popped out and he started to fall out of the car. Valarie rushed forward just in time to catch him. She had forgotten about her leg and when she had hold of him they both fell to the ground. She cried out again. Her leg really hurt. She got up, took him under the arms and dragged him up onto the shoulder of the road. He winced and groaned as if he was in pain too.

"Stop, stop," he said. Valarie dropped him and tried to catch her breath. Everything she touched felt heavy to her. She knelt down next to him.

"What happened?" she asked, still in a haze. Where was the garden? Where was her mother?

"I think we were hit. Are there any cars around?" His voice was hoarse as if he had been yelling all day.

Valarie looked up to where she had seen the truck. It was still there. "There's one over there," she said, pointing, as if David could see.

"I need you…to go check…and see if they're…all right."

Valarie nodded. She slowly got to her feet and limped to the truck. It wasn't as beat up as the car, and she was able to open the door a little easier. A man lay in the seat with his head leaning against the back of the chair. His eyes were shut and Valarie wondered why he was sleeping too. His nose was bleeding, and as she studied the face, having felt like she had seen it before. She blinked before getting closer then she gasped. She turned and tried her best to run away from the truck, but she wasn't any faster than her walk. She reached David and fell to his side.

"Is the person okay?" he asked, sounding as if he couldn't breathe.

"It's Eric."

"What?"

"Eric is in that truck." She started to cry again.

"It's okay, Val…it's okay. I need you to reach into my front pocket…"

Valarie did as she was told and pulled out his cell phone. The screen was cracked.

"Now, call 911."

She began to tap on the screen but the phone didn't light up. She turned the box over and over in her hands till she found buttons and began to push them. Nothing happened.

"It's not working!" she cried.

David raised his hand and took hers. "It's okay, just… be calm…we'll be all right." His breathing was shallow. Valarie looked around. There was no one else on the road except for the two cars, and she didn't want to go back to the truck to look for another phone.

"I need to go get help," she said, starting to rise to her feet. She groaned from the pain in her leg. David reached up and pulled on her hand. He didn't have much strength either.

"Val…stay with me…please," he said, his voice was almost pleading.

Valarie hesitated. She knew she needed to find someone, but she didn't want to leave David, nor did she know how she would get anywhere with her leg hurting the way it did.

"I need to find help," she said.

"You're hurt," he panted. "You won't…make it far. And…I don't want… to be alone…"

She knew he was right. She sat back down at his side and took his hand.

"Thank you," he mumbled.

She stayed by his side for what felt like hours, watching for traffic or any sign of life. Her mouth was unbearably dry and her head felt heavy. She leaned over and laid her head on David's chest. She could hear a slow drumming sound deep within his chest. God, she prayed, send someone to help...please...

"Val," David said.

Valarie opened her mouth to answer, but no words came out. She was too tired to reply. *Don't fall asleep*, her mind told her. *You need to stay awake in case someone comes.*

"I love you," David said. She felt his hand on her back.

"I love you too," she said. Then she closed her eyes for the third time. *Don't fall asleep*, her mind said again. *Don't fall asleep...*

CHAPTER 19

Valarie's mind woke at the feeling of someone trying to lift her. A light was flashing in her eyes though they were shut. She tried her best to open them. Someone had picked her up and she felt her body gently lay on something soft. She forced her eyes open. It was dark out. David was still lying on the ground and people in light shirts were surrounding him. Valarie realized that help had come. She felt happy inside knowing that someone had rescued them. *We'll be okay now, David*, she thought, *everything is going to be okay now*. Her eyes closed again.

Valarie felt as if something were hitting her in the head. The sound of beeping crept into her ears and she wanted to smash whatever was making the noise. She stirred. She was laying on something soft again, and her body was covered with what felt like a warm blanket. Something had hold of her hand and a voice began to speak to her.

"It's all right. You're safe, Val."

Her mind couldn't grasp what was happening, though she knew the voice was familiar. She blinked her eyes open and tried to focus on her surroundings. The walls around her were a dull color and she could see light streaming in from somewhere. A figure leaned over her, a person maybe. It continued to speak to her.

"It's all right, I'm here."

Valarie opened her mouth to answer, but no sound came out. Her throat was dry and she began to cough. Her chest felt tight and sore, as if someone had hit her with a baseball bat. Something pressed up against her lips and she felt the cool sensation of water. She felt it flow into her mouth and tried to swallow without choking.

"You're all right, Val," the voice said. She felt something take her hand again. Her skin was cold compared to whatever was touching her. She blinked again. Her father was standing over her, staring at her as if he expected her to perform some sort of magic trick.

"It's all right," he said.

"Where am I?" she asked. Her voice was so hoarse and shallow that it didn't sound like it belonged to her. She thought someone else was speaking.

"You're in the hospital, Val. You were in a really bad car accident."

Valarie could see the air bag that pushed against her face and the sight of David as he struggled to unbuckle himself. She saw Eric's lifeless face in the truck, and she remembered embracing her mother in the garden. Help had come, just like she had asked.

"David?" She asked. "Is David all right?" She tried to get up, but her father held her down. She was too weak to fight against his strength.

"It's all right, Val. Stay where you are."

"I need to see him. Is he okay?" Her throat burned with each word she spoke. She stared up at her father, wondering why he was looking at her with so much sympathy.

"Val…" He paused. He began to stroke her hair.

"Where is he?" she asked, starting to regain some strength in her voice.

"Val…David didn't make it."

Her lungs felt as if they had collapsed in on themselves. "What do you mean?" She noticed that his eyes were beginning to fill with tears.

"Val…you guys were in a really bad car accident."

"But he was fine," she said. "I pulled him out, and help came. He told me he loved me before we fell asleep."

Her father shook his head. "He didn't wake up, Val. The doctor said he had internal bleeding in his stomach. He was gone by the time paramedics arrived."

Valarie's chest hurt like it never had before. She could feel the sobs rise in her throat. "No." she said, trying to push past her dad. "I need to find him. He's okay, I pulled him out."

Her father held her down, trying to sooth her.

"No," she said, still trying to force her way out, but she was no match for him. She felt a hot tear roll down her face. David was fine, he was somewhere in the hospital and she had to find him, she had to see him.

"Val, sweetheart, you need to stay in bed," her father said. His voice was getting firm.

"No," she said.

"Val—"

"No!" She cried. Her voice cracked. Valarie heard the sound of feet rushing into the room. Something cold ran through her blood and her father held onto her as her body involuntarily relaxed.

"It's all right," he said, cradling her as if she was an infant.

She shook her head. *It's not all right*, she thought. *I need to find David. I need to.*

Valarie found herself blinking her eyes open sometime later. She didn't remember falling asleep again. She seemed to be doing that a lot lately. Her room was dark except for a desk lamp that sat to her right. She turned to look toward the window and saw her father sitting in a chair staring out the glass at something Valarie couldn't see. It was dark outside as well. She remembered him holding her, and telling her that David was gone. Was he lying? No, she told herself.

Her father wouldn't lie to her like that. But David couldn't be gone, she pulled him out, he spoke to her before she fell asleep. She shouldn't have fallen asleep. She should have kept him awake so that when help came they would have been able to save him. She shouldn't have fallen asleep.

Her father turned to her and saw that she was awake. He stood and went to her bedside.

"Hey, Val," he said. His voice was gentle. "How are you feeling?"

Valarie thought for a moment. She couldn't feel anything, in fact, she felt numb from the news she was trying to process. "What happened?"

Her father's eyes looked sad as he began to speak to her. "I'm not really sure," he said. "I was still at home when I got a call saying that you had been found on the side of the road. Someone had come across the crash and called police. They said that someone hit you from behind and the car was shoved off the road and into a tree. The impact was really hard, Val. You've suffered a few bruised ribs, and your leg is broken."

Valarie remembered the pain in her leg as she tried to open the car door. "How long have I been in here?"

"Two days."

She tried to breathe, but her chest hurt so much that she felt like she was suffocating. "What happened to David?"

Her father looked down and took her hand. Valarie didn't want him to waste time being sympathetic. She wanted to know what happened. "The impact had caused the steering wheel to push into his ribs. A few broke and basically poked his insides. He was bleeding very slowly, and by the time paramedics got to you, he was gone. I don't know how long you guys were out there…" His voice trailed off as tears welled up in his eyes again.

Valarie looked away from him. She felt the sting of her own tears and she wished that her father would leave her for a moment. David was gone? How could that be? He was going to graduate and start college and they were going to have a good summer together. All of a sudden his life is taken away? Why! Suddenly she caught a glimpse of Eric's face when she opened the truck door. David had been concerned about the other driver when all along the kid had caused the accident on purpose. He rammed into their car and drove them off the road. He hurt her, and he killed David. A rage like none other started to swell inside her. She wanted to jump out of her bed, find him and beat him till he hurt as much as she did.

"Where is he?" she asked, facing her father.

Her father shook his head. "He's probably getting ready to be buried."

"Not David," she said, hot tears were streaming down her face. "Eric."

Her father's expression changed. "How did you—"

"I saw him. I went to help him. He crashed into us on purpose. He killed David, Dad. He killed him!" Her voice cracked in anger.

"Val, you need to calm down," her father said. She felt as if it was too late to calm down. Eric had gotten in the way for the last time. He had killed her David. She was going to make sure that he would pay.

"Eric was hurt pretty bad too."

"I don't care," Valarie said.

"Wait just a minute," her father said, his voice was almost defensive. "He's in this hospital too. When his truck hit your car he was jarred forward pretty hard on the steering wheel. He didn't response to paramedics, and he's been in a coma since they brought him in."

Coma? she thought. *Wow, what karma.*

"On top of all that, he's looking at twenty to life in prison for voluntary manslaughter. Police say the crash was intentional considering his record at your school."

Valarie knew it was intentional. Prison? It would be what he deserved. *I hope he rots in there*, she thought. It was his entire fault that David was gone, all because he was a stupid kid who couldn't learn to give up. She turned away from her father again. Tears continued to stream down her face until her eye lids became heavy. She didn't want to fall asleep. She wanted to stay awake until she saw that Eric got what he deserved.

"Is there anything I can get you?" her father asked.

Valarie didn't answer. She already felt a painful longing in her heart for David. She wanted to be with him, even if that meant that she died too.

"Hello, Valarie," a tall man in blue scrubs had come into her room late the next morning. She had only been awake for a few minutes before his booming voice rang in her ears. "I'm Dr. Kohl. I've been keeping track of you since you came in. How are feeling today?"

Valarie didn't answer. She just stared at him, wondering why he was in such a good mood when David was dead.

Dr. Kohl waited for her answer. "Valarie?"

She looked away, hoping that he would leave her alone.

,"Well Valarie, you're going to be in here for a few more days, until those ribs heal up. Is your head hurting or anything?"

Valarie stared out the window.

"Valarie, I need you to talk to me so I can help you get better."

She saw her father move closer to her. "Val, what's wrong?" he asked. She didn't answer him either. She wanted everybody to leave her alone.

"Mr. Edwards, may I speak with you a moment?" The two left the room in silence and she was glad once they were gone. She stared out the window. From her position on the bed all she could see was the pale blue sky and white fluffy clouds. She wondered why the sky seemed to be in a good mood too. The whole world should be sad that David was gone. But nobody seemed to care but her.

Her father came back in a few moments later. "Val, would you like something to eat?"

She suddenly became aware of the cold, empty feeling in her stomach and realized that she hadn't eaten in two days. But she didn't care. *Let me waste away and be gone*, she thought.

Her father stared at her, waiting for her to answer. For the first time in her life, she didn't want to hide behind daddy's leg.

"Valarie, I'm Dr. Marshall, one of the hospital's counselors. How are you feeling today?" This time it was a woman, short and blonde who had come in to her room almost an hour later. Valarie was sitting up in her bed, still staring out the window. She hadn't said a word to anybody the whole day.

"Do you remember anything about the accident?" the woman asked.

Valarie had remembered it all, but she didn't say so. What did it matter now? David was gone, and so was all meaning to life.

"Why don't you tell me about David?"

Valarie turned to glare at her. How dare she speak of David? How dare she say his name? He was dead, couldn't anybody respect that? Why wouldn't anyone let her mourn in peace?

Dr. Marshall stared at her as if she was waiting for a reply. Valarie turned back to the window.

"I know you've been through an awful lot lately, and not wanting to talk is a normal sign of grief. But I'm here to help you, Valarie. It's okay to talk to me."

I don't want your help, Valarie thought. *I want to be left alone.*

The doctor turned toward her father. "Why don't you get her something to eat? I'll be back in a little while." She left without another word.

After the failed attempt to find out what Valarie wanted to eat, her father went ahead and ordered her a sandwich. Despite her will to refuse everything, her stomach growled when she saw food. He placed the tray on the bedside table and handed her the ugly brown plate. She slowly picked up the sandwich and took a bite. It felt good to finally eat something, but the food hurt as soon as it landed in her stomach. She realized that it was going to be a long road to her recovery.

That evening Dr. Marshall came back like she had said she would. But Valarie still hadn't said a word. The doctor tried asking her different questions about herself in an attempt to get her to talk, but Valarie didn't break. She stared at the window and wished she was a bird so she could fly away and be rid of everybody.

Valarie saw David lying on the ground on the side of the road. She held onto him, telling him that she loved him when Eric came up to them. He stared down at her and stared laughing. Then the sound of someone's screams had pulled her away. She looked around and saw that she was in the hospital, and the screaming was coming from her own mouth. Her father rushed to her side and held her close.

"It's okay," he said. "You're okay. It's just a dream…it's just a dream."

Valarie clung to her father and sobbed onto his shirt.

The next morning her father had helped her out of bed and into the bathroom. She hated being hooked up to all those IV tubes filling her with liquids. It made her feel like she had to pee all the time. As she got out of bed she felt her whole body ache. It made her want to fall back onto the bed. She made it to the bathroom very slowly, still limping even though her leg was in a cast. On her way back to her bed she stopped at the window. Her room was three or four stories up, for when she looked down she could see the cars parked in different lots. A few people were walking into the building and she spotted some kind of small animal near the trees across the road. *How could life continue to go on without David?* she wondered. She felt that everything in the world was all wrong.

"Good morning, Valarie." She hadn't heard anyone come in, but Dr. Marshall was speaking to her. Valarie wanted the woman to give up. She wasn't going to talk anyway.

"How are you feeling today? I see you're standing on your own."

Duh, thought Valarie. *Thanks for the obvious*. She stared out the window at the small animal and realized that it was a squirrel. It ran up a tree trunk only to turn around and run back down. It paused near the ground for a long time. She could hear Dr. Marshall talking to her, but she didn't bother to pay attention. She suddenly saw the squirrel turn and look at her. She closed her eyes. *Great, now I'm hallucinating*, she thought. The squirrel seemed to gaze at her, as if there was something he wanted to tell her. *What do you have to say?* she thought. *That everything is okay? That David is in a better place? That I need to talk to this stupid doctor like I did when my mother died?* Valarie felt tears well up in her eyes. She wished her mother was there for her. She had seen her in the garden. She had held her, and David was with her. Was he in a better place? That place that he and her mother believed in? Would her mother take care of him? Why couldn't she have stayed with them? Why did she have to come back? Then she thought of her dad. Who would he have if she had died too? He would be all alone in the giant orchard with nothing and no one. Maybe that's what the squirrel would tell her. Open up, Valarie, she heard David say, you don't have to hide it. The tears silently streamed down her face.

"All right, Valarie, I'll be back again later," Dr. Marshall said. She heard the woman's footsteps grow faint. Her breathing began to get shallow, and she spoke for the first time in three days. "I saw her."

CHAPTER 20

Dr. Marshall's footsteps stopped. "Saw who, Valarie?" Valarie was still facing the window, her gaze fixed on the squirrel. "My mother." Her father had gone to her side and helped her sit back on the bed. He covered her with the blanket and listened intently.

"When did you see her?" Dr. Marshall asked.

Valarie breathed in deep. She felt her father's hand wipe her tears. "After the crash, I was in a garden…a beautiful garden, surrounded by flowers and trees, and she was there, near a water fountain. She saw me and I ran to her and hugged her." She looked up at her dad who was fighting back tears.

"I held her, Dad," she said, speaking to him. "I held her close and she smiled at me. And David was there too."

Her father wiped his tears and looked up at the doctor as if he wanted an explanation for her illusion.

"It's quite normal to have an out of body experience in the presence of a trauma," she said. Valarie shook her head. She wished the doctor would speak English.

"You suffered a great injury, Valarie, and your body's response was to go to a place of comfort and peace. It's perfectly normal. Do you remember anything else that happened?"

Valarie nodded.

"Can you tell me? Can you start from the beginning?"

Valarie thought back to the moment she and David had been in the grove of trees. She could see them dancing to their song, and she could feel his kisses. She started talking about the impact, her head hitting the dashboard and walking through the garden. She told them about her getting out of the car, pulling David out and checking the truck to make sure the driver was all right. She felt a new flash of anger when she told them that she had seen Eric. Then she told them about falling asleep and waiting for help to come. She told them about David wanting her to stay with him. She suddenly realized that she had unconsciously listened to his heart beat for the last time.

"It sounds like you were on the side of the road all day," her father said, wiping her face then his. Valarie could tell that he felt bad that they were alone after the crash. But there was nothing he could have done for he didn't know about the accident.

"I should have stayed awake and to keep David awake. If I had done that he might still be alive," she said calmly.

"No, Valarie," Dr. Marshall shook her head. "David was hurt internally. You probably couldn't have kept him awake for very long before the blood flooded him. It wasn't your fault, and there was nothing you could have done for him."

Valarie was getting tired of horrible things happening to her and then being told that it wasn't her fault. Then whose fault was it? Who was to blame? She thought of Eric. It was his fault.

Her father took her hand and she stared up at him. "I think he's with Mom, in the place she always talked about, heaven. And I was there too," she told him.

Her father caressed her hand. "Maybe it wasn't your time to go yet."

"But he's gone, Dad," she said, starting to cry again. "He's gone and all I ever wanted was to be with him."

"Valarie, people are sent into our lives for a reason, and we don't get to choose how long they are with us, all we can do is treasure the time we have with them while they are here." Dr. Marshall's voice was soft.

She closed her eyes and shook her head then she looked back at her dad. "I loved him."

Tears rolled down her father's face. "I know you did," he said. "And I saw all the good that he did for you. I saw how he helped you with your fears and worries, and how you became stronger and braver over time."

Valarie felt her eyebrows pull together. Did he know about her anxiety?

"I prayed for a long time that God would send someone in your life to help you because I didn't know how. I saw you run outside every night and fall to your knees as if you were trying to escape something terrible."

"You knew?" Valarie asked in disbelief.

Her father nodded.

"Why didn't you say anything?" she asked.

"I didn't know what to do for you," her father answered. "I talked to doctors and the counselor we saw after your mother died, and they all said that you were suffering from anxiety attacks. They told me to try to get you to participate in things and meet some friends and not sit inside all the time. And if that didn't work they suggested for you to see a counselor. I knew you wouldn't do that, so I asked God for an alternative. When David came along and he started liking you and wanting to be with you, I thought God had finally heard me. I thought He had sent me some help even though it was in the form of an eighteen-year-old kid."

That's why you encouraged me to be with him, she thought. This whole time her father knew about her anxiety. He saw her suffer and he watched her run away from her fear every night. When she thought he was asleep in bed he was really trying to figure out how he could put an end to her problem. But all the poor man could do was plead with a Higher Power.

"I had never believed there was a God until I saw the impact that David had on you," her father continued. "He was very good to both of us."

Valarie looked down at her lap. "What am I supposed to do now?" she asked aloud.

"The only thing you can do," Dr. Marshall answered. Valarie had almost forgotten that she was still in the room. "You need to remember all the good things he said and did for you, remember that he's in a good place, and know that he loved you as much as you loved him. It's going to be a hard road from here, Valarie, but if you take one day at a time, you'll be able to look back one day and know that what you two had was special."

Suddenly a thought came to her. "When is his funeral?" she asked her father.

He shook his head. "I don't know."

"Please find out for me. I want to go."

"Val, you shouldn't leave the hospital until you're better," he said.

"Please," she said. Her voice was almost pleading.

Her father nodded. "I'll try."

Valarie checked herself out of the hospital in time to attend David's funeral, with the agreement that she would be back for more checkups and counseling. Her dad had brought her some clothes to change into and when she got home she realized she smelled like a hospital. She did her best to shower with her bruised and broken bones then dressed in the dark clothing she had worn to her mother's burial.

She wore David's necklace and tried to force back her tears. She stood off to the side as the golden brown coffin was laid in the ground. She saw Mrs. Summers cry heavily into her husband's black shirt. The man patted her back, trying to comfort his wife even though his face was wet. Valarie's heart broke for them. They lost a great kid. People she didn't know had gotten in line to lay down flowers. When it came her turn she limped to the coffin with her father by her side. She kissed the rose in her hand and threw it down. It landed silently on top of all the others. Then she limped away and walked back to her father's truck. She didn't want to stay to watch them pour dirt on the coffin.

Her house felt empty and alone, just like her heart. There was an awkward silence and tension, for grief had filled the air. Everything seemed different to Valarie, even the orchard and the furniture. It was all empty and meaningless. She wondered how she was going to take life day by day.

"Can I make you anything to eat, Val?" her dad asked, after she had changed out of her clothes. He helped her sit on the couch and stared at her as if waiting for her to break.

"No, thank you," she said politely. Her eyes stung from her tears and she could already feel the puffiness. She didn't care though, she felt as if she would never care about anything again.

Her father cooked some food anyway and brought her a plate of warm soup and bread. Valarie tried to smile at him. He was always so caring of those he loved. She ate a few bites for his comfort. As the sun began to set, her father seated himself next to her with a book. Valarie could tell he wasn't really reading, just trying to have something to busy himself with. He jumped at the sound of a knock on the door. Valarie picked up his book as he went to answer the call. He came back a few moments later with Mrs. Summers. She was still in her black dress from the funeral. Valarie scooted over on the couch to make room for her.

"I hope you don't mind my coming over," she said. Her voice was soft.

"Don't worry about that. What can I do for you?" Valarie asked, trying to comfort the woman in any way she could.

"Well, after the funeral you left before I got the chance to talk with you."

Valarie shook her head. "I'm sorry, that was rude of me."

"It's all right, dear. I understand." She sniffed. "I just want you to know that David loved you very much, and I'm glad he had someone like you with him in his last moments."

Just when Valarie thought her crying was over, she started to tear up again.

"I know there was nothing you could have done for him, but at least you stayed by him, and he didn't have to die alone."

Valarie swallowed hard. "He asked me to stay," she said.

Mrs. Summer's nodded. "I just wanted to say thank you for being a good friend to him."

"I hope I was as good to him as he was to me, ma'am," Valarie confessed.

Mrs. Summers nodded again. Valarie felt very awkward having a heartfelt conversation with her, and she would have given anything for a healed leg so she could run away. Suddenly the woman stood up. "I'll let you rest, dear," she said with a forced smile. She started for the door. "Oh," she said suddenly and turned around. She pulled what looked like a composition notebook out of her purse and handed it to Valarie over the back of the couch.

"Every school year David starts a new journal, so he will remember all that went on during the semester. I thought I would give you this one, after all, it's all about you."

That night, Valarie limped her way upstairs to her room. Her father had insisted on her sleeping on the couch in case she needed him during the night, but she said she wanted her own bed after having slept in the hospital for four days. She made it to her room, called down to her father that she was all right then shut her door and leaned against it for a while. She stared at the floor, holding David's notebook in her hand. She wondered how she was ever going to fall asleep. Her mind began to replay the events of that day. She could see the coffin, Mrs. Summers' tear-stained face, and all the people who showed up. She hadn't taken the time to meet anybody, but she didn't care. All she wanted to do now was lie down on her bed and never get up. Dr. Marshall had told her that it was normal to feel depressed after losing a loved one. Valarie knew that, but she had felt different when her mom died. She had felt like a piece was taken away from her, but now after losing David, she just felt empty. She remembered all that David had said about going to school and becoming a counselor. He had encouraged her to pursue what dreams she did have and not to let any fears get in the way. Why had David been kept from his dreams? Why did he have to die before he accomplished anything? He was so young yet so wise. He would have been a great counselor. She started to wonder if the God he served was just being selfish, if he wanted David all to himself. *Well, You got what you wanted*, she thought, *and now I'm all alone, and his parents are all alone too. Are You happy now? Are You happy that You've taken away everybody I've ever loved? Is that what You do with your power? That's as selfish as selfish can get. David didn't deserve to die. I didn't deserve to lose him. This is all one big joke to You, isn't it? Do You find this funny? Do You enjoy making people suffer for no reason and letting us feel like it's our entire fault? What kind of God are You?*

In a fit of anger Valarie threw the notebook against the wall. She limped over to her nightstand, picked up her books, and threw them one by one. She threw her pillows off her bed, her shoes that she picked up off the floor and her pencil cup from her desk. She came to the picture of her and David at his spring formal, and as she picked it up she paused. She looked down at the photo, at their happy faces. That night was the best night of her life. She had ruined it, as she ruined everything, but David was too kind to care. He helped her work through her problems and he told her he'd wait to kiss her. Valarie would never feel his kiss again, or his hand, or his warm embrace. It was gone, all gone. She stared at the picture for what felt like hours. She remembered him telling her that everything happened for a reason. For the first time in her life, she didn't want any more reasons. She didn't want to find out why she had to suffer. She didn't want any comfort or to pray to God and ask Him to help her through this rough time. All she wanted was David back. She limped over to her bed and sat down, still looking at the picture frame. Then she looked around at her messy room. Her pencils were scattered everywhere, her pillows lay on the floor, and books lay open near the wall. She spotted David's notebook and went to pick it up. She opened it to the first page and saw him sitting on his front porch, writing the words she couldn't bring herself to read. The book was two-thirds full. She almost wished his mother hadn't given it to her. But Mrs. Summers said it was all about her. She must have read it. She must have gotten a glimpse inside her son's heart and read all his thoughts and secrets. She probably knew more about Valarie than Valarie hoped anybody ever would. She stared at the first page and began to read his handwriting.

March 16, 2013

I'm unpacked and settled here in this old Georgia house. It kind of smells funny, but mom says that's because it hasn't been lived in for a while. There's a peach orchard about a mile from here, a decent walk for me to take at night. There's an old house there too, and apparently a man and his daughter live there. I wonder if I can get some free peaches.

Valarie laughed. David always was a sucker for the peaches. Then she frowned, for she realized that he never got to taste one.

March 17, 2013

My first day of school had gone better than I thought. Even though I've been to a new school more times that I can count, I still get a little nervous. But the day was fine. I've met someone, and I'll be honest when I say that I can't stop thinking about someone with short brown hair, pure blue eyes and a smile that sparkles like no other. She's very shy, shyer than anyone I've ever known.

It makes me wonder what she's been through. It turns out she's my neighbor, the daughter of the orchard owner. I found her outside in the trees, on the ground as if she was looking for something, or so she says. She's a weird thing, but I think over time I can get her to talk, and stay in one place.

Maybe over time we can become friends.

Valarie smiled. She never knew that she had a smile that sparkled. She always tried to smile through the pain. It was all she could do to try to appear normal. She picked up her pillows and set them at the head of the bed. Then she lay down to continue to read. She read until her eyes became heavy and the thought of David was flowing through her mind like a spring.

CHAPTER 21

Therapy sessions started at once a week, then one every two weeks for Valarie. She didn't like talking to someone about things in her life that felt so personal, but the doctor had recommended that she see a specialist because of the trauma she had gone through, and she didn't want to be thrown into a nut house for refusing help. She admitted to herself that she felt better after she had talked with Dr. Marshall, yet it wasn't the same as talking with David. Life simply wasn't the same without him. She read a few pages in his journal every night until she fell asleep, and she often dreamed about him. Then she woke up the next morning feeling sad that he was gone and she often spent the morning hours in her room crying before she went downstairs. A few times she awoke in the middle of the night to the sound of an ear piercing scream, then she would feel her dad shelter her in his arms and realize that she had been the one screaming. After a month or so, the nightmares began to go away. One morning she woke up and realized that she had slept peacefully and didn't spend the morning hiding in her room. That morning she found herself praying to God, asking Him to help her get through the day. Then she felt stupid for asking God for help after all the thoughts she had the night of David's funeral. She had asked her father if she could borrow her mother's Bible. He hesitated before pulling it out of his nightstand drawer, and when he handed it to her he smiled gently.

"Maybe it can help you the way it helped her," he said.

I hope so, Valarie thought. She promised she would take good care of it and found herself reading from it a little everyday. She never learned what became of Eric or his prison sentence, but she tried not to think about him, for thinking about him gave her nightmares.

Valarie found herself wandering the orchard one night. Despite the doctor's orders to keep her leg elevated, she would take her time limping through the trees. She would always stop at the tree where she and David had their first kiss. The first time going back brought her to tears, as did the second time, and the third. By the fourth time she felt like she couldn't cry anymore. She sat down and leaned against the trunk, resting her head on the rough bark. She sat for what felt like hours until her back grew stiff and she felt sleepy. She limped back home and went straight to bed.

The day after she got her cast off, she awoke early, dressed, and went downstairs. The house was quiet, and she could sense that she was alone. She wandered into the kitchen and found a small sheet of white paper on the table.

Hey Val,

I'll be out in the orchard with the workers today.
If you need anything come and find me.

Dad

Valarie went over to the coffee table where her father usually kept his date book. It was open to the day of July 29. She paused and reflected on how quickly the time had passed. David had been gone for almost two months, and she would start her senior year soon. Life had continued despite her loss. She wondered if the emptiness would ever go away. Then she realized that the car accident had prevented her father from harvesting the fruit earlier in the year. She hoped his buyers would hold out for him.

She slowly got herself something to eat then she went outside and walked all the way to the back of the orchard. Her father usually put the workers there first and worked their way up. She passed by Ricky, a tall colored man who always smiled bright; Bobby, who was short yet thin; Thomas, who always had a piece of candy in his pocket; and Mike, who would occasionally let her ride on the back of the tractor. They all greeted her with their usual enthusiasm, but Valarie could tell that they took to caution with her. Her father probably told them to be extra nice to her because of her loss. She didn't want any special attention from anyone. The world was carrying on without David, and she would have to do the same. She did her best to smile at them, but their eyes were downcast, as if they could see her pain. It made her feel awkward. Thomas offered her a piece of cherry-flavored candy, but she refused it. After she talked with them for a moment, she took a wooden barrel and began to collect some peaches from the trees. She could imagine David picking with her and saw the excitement on his face when she told him he could finally eat one. She heard footsteps getting close and for a second she assumed it was David, but when she looked up she saw Bobby. He stopped next to her and let out a sigh. Valarie could tell he was getting tired from working out in the sun all day. He began to pick some peaches with her, whistling as he usually did. Suddenly he paused and turned toward her.

"How are you doing, Valarie?" he asked. His voice was gentle.

Valarie shrugged her shoulders. "I'm good," she said. She didn't look at him for fear that he would see right through her.

"No, how are you really doing?"

Valarie was trying to avoid saying how she really felt, but she didn't see any harm in letting the man know. Her father probably told him all about the accident anyway. She sighed.

"I'm taking life one day at a time," she said. She picked up the barrel and moved a tree over. She set it on the leaf covered ground and continued picking.

"When I was twenty, I lost my first wife to a car accident," Bobby said. His voice was calm yet hoarse. Valarie stopped and gave the man her full attention.

"A drunk driver ran a red light and slammed into her truck. She died instantly." He faced her with a look of sympathy. "And you know the worst part? She was alone." His eyes traveled down as he recalled the memories. "I got a call from police one morning saying that she was in an accident. She was dead when they got to her. Of course, I was called in to identify her, and when I saw her, lifeless and gone, I ran outside and into the street. I wasn't trying to hurt myself, I was just trying to escape seeing her lifeless on a marble slab."

Valarie felt her face grow hot, and her eyes began to sting. Bobby looked up at her and to her surprise he smiled gently. "I know its hurts. It hurts more than anything. But life goes on. I had to go on, because I knew that my wife wouldn't want me to become depressed or discouraged. She would have wanted me to live as happy as I would if she were here." He left the peach tree and went over to Valarie. He patted her shoulder with his rough hand.

"She would also want me to forgive the driver that took her life," he continued. "You're a strong girl. You got so much ahead of you and so much to live for. Honor David, and live as if he was still here." He smiled one more time then he turned and left her.

Valarie stood still for a while, trying to process what he had said. Since losing David, she had become numb, lifeless, and depressed. Her counselor said it was normal, but she didn't like how it made her feel. She didn't like being alone and sad. She missed the way she felt when David was alive. She missed being happy and free. She and David had worked so hard with each other to ease the past pains and to continue on with her life despite the trials she had gone through. She knew Bobby was right. David wouldn't want her to go through the rest of her life feeling sad, and he would be the first to suggest that she forgive him. She knew that if she gave up all hope for happiness and held on to her anger and bitterness, everything David did for her would die with him. She didn't want that. She needed a piece of him, no matter how small. All she had was his journal and the memories. That would have to be enough.

She left the barrel there at the tree and started for the house. On her way she whispered aloud that she forgave Eric. Then she felt a smile spread across her face and a weight lift from her spirit. She paused for a moment and lifted her head to the sky. She shut her eyes and let the sun shine down on her for a few moments then she continued on her way. She assumed it was almost lunchtime. *I hope everybody likes roast beef sandwiches*, she thought.

Six o'clock came around that night and Valarie heard the front door open and shut. Her father was coming in for the night, and he would be hungry.

"Oh, something smells good," he announced as he entered the kitchen.

"It's a chicken casserole. It's almost ready," she said. A silence filled the house. "Are the guys staying for dinner?"

"No, they said you served them well earlier so they went home for the night." He went to the cupboard and pulled out a glass then he filled it with water from the sink.

"Oh, that's too bad; I made enough for an army," she said.

"That's all right, they can have some leftovers tomorrow. I'm going to go shower before we eat." He emptied his glass and set it in the sink.

Valarie was almost glad to not have a full house tonight. She kept going over what Bobby had told her, and suddenly a thought struck her.

"Dad?" she called. She walked into the living room and found her dad in his bedroom. He came to the doorway when she called. "Did you tell the guys what happened over the summer?"

Her father looked as if he was caught stealing. "I told them that something terrible happened to you and to take it easy on you," he confessed.

"Did you tell them David's name?"

"No."

Valarie looked down at the floor, deep in thought. If her father hadn't mentioned his name, how did Bobby know?

"Why?" her father asked.

She looked up at him. "I was just wondering. I'm going to go finish dinner."

The harvest continued until it was time for Valarie to go back to school. For the first time in all her school years, she wasn't dreading the first day. She knew what to expect, and she had a little hope knowing that this year was her last. Her father pulled up near the sidewalk and told her to call him if she needed anything. She smiled and tried to assure him that she would be all right. She got out of the truck and didn't stop to stare the building down. Instead she went straight inside, collected her necessary papers, and made it to her first class on time. When lunchtime rolled around she went through the line and got herself something to drink. She didn't feel like eating anything. Then she walked the cafeteria for a place to sit. She didn't want to sit at her usual table for fear that it would be too painful. Instead she found Emma sitting with a few girls near the window. She approached cautiously.

"Hey," she said in a meek voice.

Emma looked up at her and smiled bright. "Hey, Valarie." She scooted over to make some room. Valarie sat and let out a deep breath.

"Valarie, this is Cassie, and Jolene." She pointed to the two girls she was talking with. Valarie wondered which one was Cassie and which one was Jolene. They both had the same face and red hair.

"So how was your summer?" Emma asked.

Valarie wondered if she knew that her old lab partner was gone. "It was all right. How was yours?" She didn't want to speak about David if Emma didn't already know.

"It was all right, dull, but all right." Suddenly Emma frowned. "I heard about what happened to you and David."

Valarie swallowed hard. She braced herself.

"I just want to say I'm sorry. I know he was a good guy and that he liked you a lot…" Her voice trailed off, as if she realized that her speech was making Valarie feel miserable. She looked down at her tray of food that consisted of vegetables and dairy. The table had gone silent, and the two sisters were staring at her.

"It's all right," she said, not knowing what else to say. "Hopefully you'll have another good lab partner this year."

"What period is your lab?" Emma asked, lifting her eyes to Valarie.

"Four…I think," she said, trying to recall her schedule by memory.

A sudden light came to Emma's face as she smiled. "Want to be my lab partner?"

Valarie smiled. For the first time in a long time the smile wasn't forced. "Sure," she said. The table seemed to regain its happy energy again.

Having Emma for a lab partner wasn't so bad, but Valarie was glad when the school day came to its end and her dad came for her at four. The ride passed by as usual: her father asking her how her day went and she asking him the same question. She could honestly say that her day went fine.

After dinner that evening, Valarie stood over the kitchen sink washing the dishes, listening to the radio as she worked. She started humming along with the music when she suddenly stopped as the song became familiar to her. She gasped. Her lungs grew tight and she felt as if she was hit in the stomach. The memories came flooding into her mind. She picked up a dish and realized that her hands were shaking. She hadn't listened to the song since she and David had danced to it in the trees the day he died. She took the towel, quickly dried her hands then went into the living room. She saw her father sitting on the couch, reading his book. She tried her best to calmly tell him that she needed some fresh air. Then she was out the door. The sun was beginning to set, but she didn't stop to admire its colors. She hurried down the steps and went into the orchard. After walking past the fourth or fifth row she couldn't take the shaking anymore. She broke into a run and made her way to the very end of the orchard before tripping over her feet and landing face first in the dirt. She began to cry as she pushed herself off the ground and sat on her feet. She tried to control her sobs as she brushed her face and arms clean of dirt.

"Are you okay?" a small voice asked.

Valarie looked up. A little girl, no older than five years old, was standing near the tree line. She held a CD player in her small hands and a pair of old-fashioned headphones sat on her head over her short blonde curly hair. She stared at Valarie with a calm look on her face. Valarie was taken by surprise. Was she hallucinating?

"Yeah," she said. "I'm okay."

"I saw you fall. Did it hurt?" the girl asked. Her voice was sweet yet curious.

Valarie wondered how the child could hear her over the music in her ears. "A little."

"It hurts when I fall, see?" She held her CD player in one hand and with the other she lifted up her blue jean skirt to reveal a band aid on her knee. "My daddy put that there," she said, tapping the band aid with her small finger. She let go of her skirt. "It feels better now. You will feel better in a little while too. My daddy can get you a band aid." The child became silent and stared at Valarie again. Where had she come from? Valarie didn't recall any children living close by, not for another mile or two. Had the little girl walked a whole mile from her house on her own? Valarie stood and wiped her face. "Where did you come from?" She asked in a soft voice.

The girl turned and pointed behind her. "That house, up there." Valarie knew she was talking about David's house.

"You live there?" she asked the girl.

"Yes." The girl said. "My daddy and I just moved in today." She smiled, revealing her tiny baby teeth.

"Today?" Valarie said aloud. Mr. and Mrs. Summers were gone? Moved? Why hadn't they told her they were leaving? She would have wanted to say good-bye.

"Is this your house?" the girl asked.

Valarie nodded.

"Are these your trees?"

"Yes."

The girl looked up at her surroundings. "I like it," she said, smiling again.

Valarie thought of the look on David's face when he said the exact same thing about the orchard. She almost smiled.

"Does your daddy know you're here?" she asked.

The girl shook her head, her headphone staying in place. "No," she said. "He's busy in the house. It's too hot in the house for me."

Valarie's stomach dropped. She wondered if the girl's father was worried sick about her. "Let's take you home so your daddy doesn't get worried." She approached the little girl and the girl began to walk with her, her little feet walking twice as fast to keep up.

"Will you tell my daddy to turn on the cold air?" she asked.

Valarie smiled. "Yeah, I'll ask him for you." She began to walk the all-too familiar route to the old bed and breakfast.

It would sure be weird to set foot on that old porch. "What's your name?" she asked.

"Toni." The girl answered. "What's your name?"

"Valarie."

"Can I come back to the trees tomorrow, Valarie?" Toni asked.

Valarie looked down at the young girl and saw a sparkle in her innocent blue eyes. She smiled. "Maybe," she said. "You'll have to ask your daddy."

The little girl nodded her head and continued to walk with her toward the house. Valarie knew that the child was right, she would feel better in a little while.